C.R. Clarke is a thirty-year veteran of the film industry, having worked on more than sixty movies. His love of writing first birthed from discovering an ability to write poetry despite being dyslexic. Poetry became stories, and through his endeavours, he has all but cured his debilitating affliction.

The Puppet Tears is the second novel he has written, and the first to be published, with many more in the pipeline to follow.

For my uncle, John, whose smile will be missed … And my mother, Jean, for raising me right.

C. R. Clarke

The Puppet Tears

AUSTIN MACAULEY PUBLISHERS™

LONDON * CAMBRIDGE * NEW YORK * SHARJAH

A CIP catalogue record for this title is available from the British Library.

ISBN 9781398473089 (Paperback)
ISBN 9781398473096 (ePub e-book)

www.austinmacauley.com

First Published 2022
Austin Macauley Publishers Ltd ®
1 Canada Square
Canary Wharf
London
E14 5AA

I would like to thank my partner, Zoë, for her patience and resilience during this process. My almost mother-in-law, Janet, for her honest feedback, and to Sue from across the way, for the same. Thank you. x

Poppet: *noun*—a small cloth effigy, usually in human form, used in sorcery, witchcraft, and sympathetic magic.

Witchcraft: *noun*—the use of magic, pagan or occult, to affect change to suit the needs or desires of the practitioner.

Wicca: *noun*—a nature-oriented religion having rituals and practices derived from pre-Christian religious beliefs, typically incorporating modern witchcraft practices of a benevolent kind.

'For the words of a vow are sacred not only to men and the angels, but among the demons as well.'

Howard Schwartz.

Chapter One

The End

SHE'D FOUND MY DRAWER. She'd found my fucking drawer!

I didn't find out until I'd returned from a trip into town to purchase materials, and she confronted me. But in retrospect, I 'had' noticed a shift in the energies earlier in the day.

I guess, I must have forgotten to lock it? But why 'would' I lock it? She never went down there.

Marianna always told me my basement workshop 'freaked her out', so what the fuck was she 'doing' down there, snooping around—suspicious bitch!

But I was sure it was going to be okay, certain I'd be able to correct it. I'd 'corrected' far greater hiccups to my plans before, so I felt positive, that with little time and effort, I could do so again.

I stood in my basement workshop in the aftermath of the confrontation, the air felt cold and unwelcoming.

She'd tried to colour me as some brand of 'weirdo', but I remember feeling surprised that I found myself struggling to care. I guess, I'd just become so certain of the path of my beautiful life that I'd forgotten how to be grateful for what I had and what I was on the cusp of losing.

I could hear her walking around above me, her agitation palpable. I just stood quietly in the post-storm calmness, listening.

The woody stab of her heals made such a crack through the kitchen floorboards above my head. Amplified by the un-dampened slabs of open-planking, it was loud enough to disturb the dead—but it was a sound, over time, I'd grown to love.

I would often just sit silently beneath her, lights off, watching her busy shadow break the blades of light cutting between each board, just listening to her potter about—doing her thing.

Each crack of those stiletto'd heals would manifest an image of her tight, high-set calves into my mind. A consistent reminder of the prize I'd managed to contrive into my life.

Those perfect calves were her best feature, and take it from me, the competition for that particular crown was fierce. But they 'were' her best feature, aided by the crazy sexy shoes she wore, and the way they would force those sublime fillets of muscle into fists.

God, yeah—those legs, those 'incredible' legs.

Marianna had the most amazing legs. Even when she was much younger, she'd had the best legs of any girl in high school.

Of course, they were different then—far less race-horse—not yet toned from living a life. A flat-shoe'd softness to their awkward, teenage gait. But still, in the eyes of every fizzy-dicked kid in high school, they were great legs, and right up until that moment she discovered my fucking 'life-box', they were all mine.

I looked down into the chaos that used to be my drawer of spells. Everything I'd ever 'set' had been undone, 'she'd' undone it, and she'd also taken her poppet, the one I'd meticulously crafted to represent 'her' in my 'life-path-adjustments'.

The poppet of me was still there, tossed back into the drawer-like garbage. I think I'd actually felt a shift in my inner being around the time she must have thrown it.

The ribbon and broken threads that had bound the dolls lay on the ground. I could almost sense the revulsion she must have felt when she ejected them from her fingers, simply by the way they lay—discarded.

Or maybe I was simply picking up the negative energies she'd shed when she'd repelled them from her hands?

Yeah, that's it—I remember now—I could taste the negative fizz flavouring the aura of the room.

Things above me had gone quiet. I looked around at all of my marionettes, hanging limp from their stands, facing me.

They seemed to be watching, looking on events with interest, observing my torment with mildly disapproving eyes.

I could hear her in the kitchen again, the crack of the heals had returned, but the perfect-10 legs images were failing to manifest in my mind as they usually would?

The rhythm of her walk seemed subtly different to normal—impatiently urgent, irked, the heaviness of her stomp hailing her displeasure.

I quickly scooped the decades of ruined work into my bin, carefully placing the poppet of me to one side.

The drawer was clear for the first time in two decades and looked as empty as I felt.

I needed to secure a different 'life-box' and start all over again—and fast, before it all wore off, and she realised that she'd never actually loved me in the first place.

I decided to make a new poppet that very night while she slept. The midnight hours—my favourite time to work. No distractions. No interruptions. Just me and my 'craft', controlling the destinies of those around me to hone a life where I am king. A fair and suitable payback for a childhood of unfair ridicule and social invisibility—wouldn't you say.

I checked the jars on my shelf…Yes. I still had some Temazepam left. I would spike her night-time tea that evening. Thirty milligrams would usually do it—if she hadn't had a drink—I saw no point in delaying.

And after it had kicked in, I'd make a start. It would usually only take about half an hour before she would slip under.

I ran through my mind what I needed to gather together: an item of her clothing, a lock of her hair—I realised I could probably secure that from the brush in the bathroom. I didn't want to risk her noticing a step in the painstakingly maintained hemline of those tumbling, honey-blonde tresses that did so much to excite my heart.

I walked across to check another drawer, the one I kept my 'stuff' in.

I took out the parchment and the ink I'd need to bind the doll to Marianna, and the cloth and cotton to stitch around it.

But Jesus, what a fucking waste. The poppet she'd removed was a masterpiece. I'd obsessed over making it for days back when I was just sixteen—nearly twenty years earlier.

The one of me was purely functional and had quite literally been thrown together. But the time and care I'd taken in crafting the poppet of Marianna, I guess must have directly reflected my desire to bind her to my lonely existence.

I can recall the sheer effort and patience it took. It was such a long time ago now, but my memories are still as clear as glass.

We had all finished high school just a few months previous, and a chance encounter had presented me with an opportunity that had eluded me for years—

—I'd climbed aboard the Number 17 bus that ran every half hour into town and made my way towards the back through the stale, bubble-gum sweetness of the shared air. And there she was, sat before me—Marianna Pascal—the one and only thing on this dull, pointless planet that I'd ever truly wanted. Already on board, near the back where the cool kids sat. Perched like a Hollywood starlet next to Kirsty Green.

They had been best of friends for as long as I can remember, living just two doors apart on 'Cope Street'. Nos 15 and 19.

Both their houses had red doors, the only two on that road that did, and once the finish of school life had robbed me of any more opportunities for close contact, I would sit across from her house, in the frigid darkness of the winter evenings, simply watching, hoping for even the briefest of glimpses of her limitless beauty.

But suddenly, there she was, sat on the bus before me. It felt akin to fate, or my wishes answered.

I can see it emblazoned in my thoughts like it was yesterday—the two of them were swapping news as vibrantly as they ever had, and I wandered up and said 'hi', smiling my pleasure at seeing her beautiful face again.

But she blanked me—they both did. But truth be known, it only really bothered me that Marianna had.

Both her and Kirsty just looked through me as though they'd never seen me before. But I'd sat behind Marianna in Mr Harris' English class for the previous four years, yet she didn't even seem to know I fucking existed.

I slotted into the seat right behind them, despite the bus being close to empty.

She and Kirsty rocked forwards into a huddle, giggling like children—probably at me, and how weird it was that an apparent stranger had the sheer 'audacity' to be courteous towards them.

It angered me that sometimes, Marianna could be so cold, so hurtful. But her beauty and elegance were God-given and transcended all of those flaws, and I wanted her, I wanted her in my life. Besides—those flaws—they could be 'adjusted'.

I took a pair of scissors furtively from my pocket and took a look around…And by luck, or by fate, we were the only three people in the rear section of the bus.

I bided my time, patiently awaiting a suitable distraction.

Then, it came—in the form of a new display of 'trendy-for-a-month-then-chuck-it' clothing hanging in the window of the Dorothy Perkins on Potter's Lane.

I remember thinking the clothes looked cheap, and tacky, but Marianna had that knack of being able to pluck from tat and produce an outfit that had an air of greater expense.

Perhaps it was more to do with the 'way' she wore them, or how 'good' she looked—or possibly both? But that girl could've threaded her long, sylph-like limbs into old potato sacks and somehow made them look sophisticated.

But cheap, gaudy tat or not, it distracted them, so I took my chance and oh-so-gently hooked my finger beneath a stray lock of her velvety hair, then slowly, closed the blades around it.

My whole face winced at the very real possibility that I might get caught. Images of the backlash that would result from such an outrage strobed through my thoughts: the passing whispers of 'fucking freak', and the beatings from the town's hard kids. But I twisted my fingers hard into the loops of the shears to stifle any tell-tale 'snip'—then cut.

The soft lock fell from her beautiful head and draped my forefinger.

I carried it carefully to my pocket, passing the curiosity of my nose along the way.

The silky ribbon of blonde perfection lying across my fingers smelled so good: a mixture of high-end hairspray, some brand of citrus scent that seemed expensive, and simple, cell matter kept in the peak of physical health. A combination that perfectly serenaded the images of her timeless beauty that had for so long taken up permanent residence in my mind and sent my eyes rolling in rapture.

I didn't begin crafting her poppet until a good month after, once the hair had lost enough of its 'Marianna-ness' to enable me to free it from the covet of my fascinated fingers.

Over that most fantasy-filled of months, I fell in love with that lock of hair.

Things above me had gone disconcertingly quiet. I hung in the uncomfortable silence of the workshop for a while, then decided to climb the stairs and see what shape my life was in and assess how much work I needed to do...

I arrived at the top of the staircase that rose to the kitchen. I hung behind the door in the musk of the cellar, my forehead pressed up against the cold grains of the timber, trying desperately to think of an opener to a conversation I'd always hoped I'd never have to have.

I gripped the handle in readiness, then calmly opened the door—trying in vain to play down the gravity of recent events by forcing calm into my countenance.

I stepped from the mildly damp atmosphere into the freshness of the kitchen.

The smell of the previous evening's Bolognese still hung in the air. Marianna was such an amazing cook, but of course she was—she was perfect.

She was stood at the sink with her back to me, fiddling around with something or other.

She didn't seem to realise I'd materialised, so I called to her—apologetically. "Marianna?"

She jumped at the sound of my voice and spun around—looking halfway between guilty and afraid.

She gazed at me like I was some kind of a threat to her innocence. I could see she was fighting to decide if she trusted me or not.

Marianna thrust her hands out towards me. "What *is* this?" she insisted.

Her right hand held a pair of scissors, ironically, the exact same scissors I'd used all those years previous to crop the lock from her head. They were kept in the kitchen drawer—was that a sign?

Her other hand held the poppet she'd removed—the one representing her—opened-up at one of the side seams, dried herbs and flowerheads spilling from the opening into her delicate hand.

I looked into her eyes, they were expectant, awaiting my response…

She thrust her insistent hands towards me again, then I noticed, her fingers held the piece of parchment that had bound her to the doll. She'd removed it, and in so doing, broken the bond. The link to it manipulating her life.

I stumbled over my tongue, I could find no words to say that wouldn't make me sound guilty, or insane.

My clueless shoulders lifted, wordless lips pawing at the uncomfortable air.

I looked into the stern adamance galvanising her face, her sultry, 'Isabelle Adjani' mouth hanging open, displaying her confusion and abhorrence.

18

It was plain to see in her eyes, she didn't know precisely what it was she held in her hands, but I knew she'd seen enough Hammer movies to throw a pretty fair guess at it.

I finally managed to speak. "It's nothing. It's really nothing," I spluttered. "I was just messing about. Like a game. That's all," I said.

Was that it? Was that the best I could fucking come up with? Maybe the look in her eyes that was incinerating my self-respect was right, maybe I 'was' a complete loser.

The corners of her mouth buckled in disgust. "Jennifer's right, you are bloody weird," she said.

That bitch Jennifer Coulier! She was a 'Wiccan' and used to laughably refer to herself as a 'White Witch', but there's no such fucking thing.

I was Wiccan myself once, and if you truly believe in the 'Rede', and the 'Rule-of-Three', then there can be no such thing as 'White Witch'. It's just a monica these flowing-gown-wearing, pierced-nose tossers use to alleviate the fears of the ignorant.

But she did have knowledge, and that made her dangerous to someone like me—she'd have to be 'removed'.

Marianna stared back at my stumbling inability to explain it all away.

The look on as her face slowly morphed from disgust, to mocking contempt. Then softened to some strange form of pity I couldn't quite read. "What did I ever see in you?" she asked, rhetorically and out loud to crush me—and it worked.

It was all wearing off far too quickly; I was in danger of losing everything I'd worked for.

Her puckered brows softened above her 'Gene Tierney' eyes. She seemed a foot taller. "Is this supposed to make me love you?" she said—turning her despondent hands to flash the deconstructed doll.

I forced a frown. "Nooo. It's not like that. It's j-just, a s-s-symbolic thing," I stuttered, "you *do* love me, you *know* you do," I insisted. "It's just a game, a s-s-s-superstition thing. That's all." But I could see my stuttering words did nothing to convince her.

Her lower lids flickered, licking at the edges of her turquoise and sky-blue-flecked irises.

I watched her auditing her scrambled feelings. "Jennifer told me there might be something like this somewhere in the house," she said. "She told me that you and me, just never seemed to fit. And that she could *tell*—our relationship had somehow been *forced*."

Jennifer's fucking bitch-face flashed into my flaming mind. Anger nearly split my chest open, and I had to fight hard not to show it.

But my annoyance had given me back my voice. "A-And you believe that?" I asked—scathing. "You actually think a stupid doll can make you feel, or-or do things that you don't actually want to?"

I faked a mocking laugh to embarrass her into submission. But it was hard—ridiculing the one and only thing I'd ever loved. A person I hadn't shared so much as a single crossed word with in over two decades.

I watched her clawing at her thoughts, jostling between Jennifer's words, and mine.

She looked down at the torn-off square of parchment, turning it in her slender fingers.

I wanted to snatch it from her hand. In the cold, unforgiving light of everything, it even started to look bizarre and creepy to me.

"I don't know 'what' to think," she said—her voice racked with disappointment. "I think I need my own space for a bit."

She hung in her preposition for a few seconds, then turned resolute. "Yes, I need to go away, I need some space. Space to think. I—" She released as sigh. "I'm going out…I don't think I'll be back until tomorrow."

She crossed the kitchen, avoiding eye contact and made her way up the open flight of stairs above me, pressing the knife of her hand between her thighs to close the open hem of her skirt—like a shy whippet, tail curled between its legs.

Feeling utterly powerless, I hung below the staircase, paralysed by the moment.

I could hear her packing, but it sounded way more than just one night's worth. I didn't know what to do, I'd frozen.

I turned to look over by the sink, but she'd taken the poppet upstairs with her.

I started to feel a pre-emptive form of shame and embarrassment at the conversations she was almost certainly going to be having centred around that bastard doll.

I turned my gaze to the flat, slab of floor and its relative uncomplication to collect my thoughts. What the hell was I going to do? I'd gone from having all of the power, to having none. And all because of that fucking interfering stain on my life—Jennifer 'Bitch' Coulier.

I decided there and then, I would honour her interference by unleashing all of my worst knowledge. And no shop-bought, moon-encrusted, cheap-ass amulet was going to do anything to stop what I was going to raise, and I wanted her to be thinking of me, when she came face-to-face with what I was going to send her way.

Marianna made her way back down the stairs again; her footsteps sounded softer.

She dropped off the final step into the kitchen and stopped. She'd changed into jeans, a t-shirt and soft, flat-shoes. Dressed down—probably to show me she cared little for me to be proud of her.

She was carrying her large Vitton bag and the matching vanity case.

She hung in the pregnancy of the uncomfortable silence for a short time…All I could do was look on—awaiting my sentence.

"Listen, Samuel," she said, softly, "I—I don't know how I feel about any of this. I won't lie to you, it's freaked me out a bit. Well, a *lot*."

She lifted her face from the floor to look directly at me. Her eyes were somehow pitying. "It's not over, okay, but I need some time to think. Think about stuff, about *us*."

Her brows crimped sympathetically; I must have looked pathetic. She winced an insipid smile. "Okay?" she asked—checking I understood how much my inability to lock a cunting drawer had fractured my world.

I nodded like a berated child. I'd received my sentence, and I felt as hollow as a cave.

A taste of stomach acid climbed the back of my throat. "Okay," I said, from somewhere outside of myself.

She flashed an empty smile and turned to leave through the back door.

I heard her engine start, the inline-four hum vibrating through the deep, sandstone walls of the cottage. 'Our' cottage.

The gravel crackled as she drove past the house. Then with a swelling rasp from her exhaust, she was gone.

Chapter Two

The Marking of Jennifer Coulier

I WEPT—the way I wept when my mother passed away. But don't get the wrong idea, I never loved Mother, I was just used to her being there for me.

I guess, I wept more for the change and the feelings of emptiness than anything else. Shedding selfish tears for the new void in my life that her passing had left me with.

It's sometimes difficult for me to even remember what she looked like, but if I try hard enough, the images eventually resolve into something vaguely familiar.

If Marianna was to be considered a goddess among women, then my mother was the polar opposite: An owl-faced woman with heavily lined, duffel-bag lips. Thin, with a bowed, knobbly body. Hunched and devoid of a single straight line.

I'd only really ever known her broken and bent from a soul-destroying life of cleaning work. An existence looking down at the floors she mopped, and the shelves she wiped, until her body was no longer able to stand tall enough to see the stars that do so much to fill the human mind with dreams, wonder and awe and create in us a desire to forge a better life.

That observation alone established my love and appreciation of the skies that crowned my world and instilled in me a desire to craft an existence I 'wanted' to live—and for that, and that alone—I was thankful to my mother.

I was just nine years old when she died, and on the day, we lowered her beneath the frost-hardened soil and out of mind, a throng of tenuous family members I'd always struggled to find common ground with crowded around my self-centred sorrow the way herds of Pachyderm surround a baby elephant when the lions move in.

A valuable lesson was learned that day—my actions can influence those around me—and from that moment on, I observed.

I watched, with interest, the mechanics of the world reciprocate around me, and wrote down what I saw—indexing ways my interactions might ultimately contrive my desires.

But there were obvious limitations to how much my hamming up of life could do to waylay the problems of not being one of the cool kids. And that most gaping of holes, I eventually filled with the use of witchcraft and black magic.

But the day Marianna left—that was different. My tears were true and ran with good reason, baptising the crimson regret in my cheeks.

After the door slammed, and the roar of the engine subsided, the screaming silence left by her absence could have split my eardrums, as well as my heart.

I mourned for the rest of that day, and the day after.

An arm's length semi-circle of beer bottles peppered the floor of the window end of my grief hole couch.

Every flat surface between there and the downstairs bathroom displayed the same.

But my need to frequent that pissed-up haze soon wore off, and three pints of water and a goodish night's sleep later, I woke to re-focus my desire to get Marianna back.

But first—I needed to know where she'd gone.

I searched the house for clues to where she might be, but there 'were' none. She'd taken everything she'd need for daily life with her.

But patience would be the key to accomplishing this most crucial of goals, so I waited until 6:30 that evening—close to the cusp of when the skies would begin to darken at the tail end of summer—and then I began…

I threaded myself into my midnight-blue top with the hood, grabbed a bag of salt from the kitchen cupboard, then passed by the shed to collect a trowel—things I'd be needing later for a different task.

I jumped into my car and set off to find which particular brand of whore was keeping Marianna from me.

I made for Kirsty's first—hers being top of my list of likely places she would go.

She still lived in the house on Cope Street, except by that time, it belonged to her. It must have been part of her inheritance when her parents passed on—her being an only child.

The journey there could be made in one of two ways. I chose to take the single track lanes that traversed the wooded outcrops of the northern end of town.

It gifted me the time I needed to plan my actions, and there was no denying, the idyllic scenery flashing past the windows had an undoubted calming effect on my mood that aided thought.

The reality was, it had been a good long time since I'd had to plan, or perform any 'real' magic. I'd had everything I wanted around me for so long, I'd not needed to.

It began to feel like old times again, a rush of excitement in my belly and a strange feeling of power that an ability to influence the world around you can give.

Eventually—I arrived.

I reached up and swung both sun visors down, sat high in the seat to obscure my face and traversed the roads surrounding Kirsty's house.

But after several passes, I came up empty. Marianna's car was nowhere to be seen.

I parked up to re-group my thoughts.

An image of Marianna thrusting the doll towards me flashed into my mind. *The doll*, I thought, *of course*.

I set off again for the far side of town, to where that fucking 'White Witch' slut Jennifer lived.

I turned into the road that ran past her complex of apartments. She owned one of the top floor flats that overlooked the communal gardens to the rear, so was unable to see the main road—ideal.

I slowed and cruised silently past, and there it was—Marianna's white, soft-top Audi—parked up outside the gates to the complex's parking area.

I quickly drove past to avoid being seen and parked up in a quiet cul-de-sac around the corner.

The engine fell silent, and I sat—waiting.

The engine ticked and popped as the crank case cooled.

The interior gradually chilled until it matched the outside temperature, then continued to drop along with it, as day gradually morphed into dusk.

I leaned forwards and turned my eyes through the top of the screen. The sky was beginning to pepper with resolving stars that had lay hidden in the brightness of the summer skies.

The road I'd parked on was on the opposite side from town, so I reckoned there'd be little chance of either of them passing that way.

The streetlights fizzed on one at a time and gradually warmed into a tungsten glow, painting the concrete paving a soft, apricot-orange.

I waited, patiently, until the last of the sunlight had left the skies and all was dark, save for the conical haze of the streetlights. A two-hour period of stillness and reflection, I'd sat quietly within to ready myself for the work that lay ahead of me.

I alighted the car, pulled the hood up over my head and stowed the trowel in my waistband.

I set off, trying to walk in that chicken-necked way dumb kids did at the time to try and look fashionably criminal. It was by far the best way to blend into an area so close to the Harper Estate—our particular town's cluster of social housing.

Every place has an end to be avoided by the innocent and law-abiding, and the Harper Estate definitely wasn't considered the de-rigueur area of Bradlington.

I saw the Audi ahead of me—she was still there.

I looked around for Jennifer's piece-of-shit Renault 2CV. I saw it, parked-up badly in her apartment's designated spot, abandoned spanning two spaces. All of the amulets and 'look-at-me', 'here-I-am' piercings in the world couldn't make her into a good driver.

I walked slowly past to scout the lay of the land. Everything seemed quiet and still. Again—perfect.

I doubled back at the end of the road to pass by again. There was still no one around, so I grabbed my chance.

I slipped through the gate to the apartment complex and scurried across the dimly lit parking area to the main doors.

There was no one else around; it was strangely quiet, almost like my actions were being assisted.

I stepped back and scanned the entrance—trying to channel Jennifer. "Where would you bury it?" I asked out loud.

There were just two possibilities I could see: small flowerbeds that flanked the doorway, and two, faux-Grecian concrete urns sat either side.

I figured the urns would be visited by the groundsmen far too frequently to be a viable option, so I decided to go for the beds.

I took a quick peek through the chequered wires of the fire-proof glass, to make sure no one was coming down the stairs, then taking the trowel from my belt, I began to dig the small beds flanking the entrance.

I scooped at the soil frantically, twisting my head around like a nervous bird, looking for anyone that might approach, asking questions for which I had no answers.

The left bed came up empty, so I quickly brushed the soil back into the hole and shuffled across the opposite side.

Another quick peek through the door and I began digging again.

Almost instantly—on the third or fourth thrust of the trowel—I hit something hard.

I jabbed the tool into the ground a few times. It rang bright and glassy.

I quickly dug around the object with my hands and scooped up an old jam jar caked in mud.

I stabbed the trowel a few more times into the soil around the hole to check it was the only one, then filled it in again, patting it flat so no one could tell I'd ever been there.

I hurried back to the car clutching my find, opened the boot and tossed the trowel in.

I lifted the jar into the warm, orange light and wiped my thumb across the glass…And there it was—a 'Witches-Bottle'—a glass jar covered in runic script, housing nails, razor blades, slithers of rusted tin, pins, wire, hooks, needles. Filled to the brim with Jennifer Coulier's paranoid piss, buried by the entrance to her home to protect her from the ill-will of others—and I'd just removed it.

I grinned at the prospects, then cracked the rusted lid and unscrewed it, placing the open jar down on the pavement.

I tore open the bag of salt and poured the crystals into the pot until a woof of pungent, yellow fluid spilled over the sides. Then with all of my hate-spitting, boiling inner resentment—I stamped the thing out of existence.

Jennifer's defecant soaked my shoes, and I briefly allowed the fantasy it was her blood to feed my loathing.

I felt the hate in my face morph into a smirk. I felt justified and ready for the sickly sweet taste of retribution.

I would invoke 'Aishma', a Judeo demon of wrath, and Jennifer Elizabeth Coulier—Arian, born March 22nd—would almost certainly be thinking of me on the night it came for her.

I left happy and headed for the next location on my agenda.

At that time, there were excavation works going on over at the church in Aspley—a small but neat village tagged onto the outskirts of the main town that looked more like a movie set than anything real.

I'd seen a piece about it in the local paper. Some long-nosed, do-gooding locals had objected, deeming the work to be somehow sacrilegious. But I'd been meaning to pass that way and see if there was anything of use worth scavenging, and I was now in possession of the perfect reason to pay the location a visit.

I parked up on the lane around the corner, turned off the ignition, and everything fell into pitch blackness.

My fingers chased the cylinder of my torch around the glovebox. I took it into my hand, slammed the lid and rose from the car.

My softening pupils widened to the moonless night as I nudged the door shut.

The sky shone midnight-blue above and behind the ebony silhouettes of the surrounding hills and trees.

They looked flat, cut-out, like a decoupage diorama. Nothing felt real.

Juddering torchlight illuminated my path through the lanes as I made my way around to the covered entranceway that led into the church grounds.

The heavy, striated grains of the oak timbers popped in the torchlight as I approached it, worn deep into trenches by the constant buffeting of the inclement weather that naturally peppered such an exposed location.

The church itself sat atop a hillock and lorded over the nearby village.

The hinges complained as I swung the gate open, hailing my arrival to those that slept beneath the soil.

I shone the light around the graveyard, looking for clues to what I was seeking.

The fan of light burned through the darkness, meandering over the forgotten monuments to the old and unfortunate: a sea of praying angels, Saxon crosses, Celtic knots, and staggered rows of listing headstones interrupted the persistent beam.

Then, the light washed across something not in keeping, daring to shout its existence in defiant, vibrant yellow from the farthest side of the cemetery grounds.

I strained to see through the thin layer of hanging mist that the night air had lifted from the soil.

I could just about make it out—the yellow thing calling to me from the farthest side—was a digger.

I made my way through the cemetery towards it. I could hear the whisperings of the dead as I walked through the sea of fractured and fallen gravestones, passing news of my approach as I traversed their subterranean dormitory. I attempted to tread lightly so I could hear what they were saying, but my efforts were met by an invoked wind that rustled the spiny leaves of the surrounding yew bushes.

The digger was parked at the edge of large area of excavated burial ground. It was being cleared of forgotten graves, swept aside to make way for new arrivals—those who still had members of the living to weep for their absence.

I spun the torchlight towards the church. All of the old headstones had been stacked respectfully around the perimeter of the walls.

I paced the upturned soil, painting the ground with the disc of light.

My feet kicked at the clods of earth, trying to find what I was there to collect.

Then my kicks began to turn up what I was seeking.

My knees thumped onto the un-desecrated ground, and I clamped the torch beneath my chin.

I began sifting through the clumps of clotted soil, extracting slithers of rotting wood from the greasy mud.

I gathered a healthy pile together and began to check each piece.

I began to find what I was looking for and started twisting them from the soft, decayed timbers.

I opened my fingers beneath the torchlight to inspect my hoard—a cluster of coffin nails lay in the muddy palm of my hand, rusted thin to jagged points and stained black by the peat of a hundred decomposing corpses.

I pocketed my find and rose to leave—apologising for the interruption to those prostrate beneath my soft footsteps.

Eventually, I arrived back at the cottage, slapped the kettle on and made some tea to clear the lingering remnants of my hangover.

I quickly tidied away the cityscape of beer bottles that peppered the house, to clear my mind and help draw a close to that most unfortunate of chapters of my hitherto ideal existence. Then it was time to do some work.

A soft knot formed in my gut as I descended into the musk of the cellar; it transported me back to that moment my happiness ended and I was presented with such an enormous problem to solve.

31

But I couldn't allow myself to dwell on it anymore. 'Onwards and upwards' as they say—whoever 'they' are?

My hand felt around the dark for the switch of the angle-poise. I clicked it on and was greeted by all of my marionettes hanging from their stands, facing me, their little faces under-lit by the soft light bouncing off the cedar worktops.

They dangled around the perimeter of my bench, patiently awaiting my return, and at that moment in time, it was easy to imagine that they were the only real friends I had.

One lay in pieces on the table-top, morbidly dismembered, looking akin to the victim of a terrible accident. *Another omen?* I wondered. Possibly, but I couldn't be certain.

They were parts for a commission piece that I desperately needed to finish and looked macabre in its deconstructed state, as macabre as the work that lay ahead of me like a darkened path through unfamiliar forest.

It needed to be handed over to the client in a little more than a week, but I had 'far' more important things to do 'that' night, so I brushed the pile of limbs aside and made a start.

My drawer of 'stuff' was still pulled out from earlier in the day.

I walked over and tore of a small, foot-sized piece of homemade parchment and carried it back to my desk.

I settled on my stool, flattening out the slither of paper, then leaned across to load my CD player with Penderecki's *Polymorphia*, a piece of music I would always play when setting a curse. Broodingly dark, it never failed to put me in a suitable frame of mind to raise the right kind of energies.

The nib of my pen ruptured the surface tension of the ink in my antique well. The liquid onyx sucked up the split to the reservoir, and I was ready to begin.

In all such work, my markings were meticulously made. I took great pride in my craft, using the same levels of care and attention that I would when fashioning my marionettes.

That bland slither of parchment gradually transformed into a document detailing who Jennifer Coulier was and what was to become of her.

After a good hour, I carefully art-worked the final crowning piece of the curse—the 'Seal of Asmodeus'—the key to unleashing and bringing forth 'Aishma', the underworld prince of lust and wrath.

All being well, I would set it the following day, the gates would be opened, and from that moment forth, all would be relentlessly inevitable.

I took to my bed for the night; it would be an early start, everything was ready.

It would often occur to me—that in many ways—the life of an occultist drew many similarities to the life of a private detective. At least, it did to the way they were portrayed on film.

I was back in my car again, parked up on the street that Coulier's apartment complex was on.

I had a clear, unhindered view of the door to the building, and I waited and waited and waited some more…

It was 6:15 in the morning, and I'd been there since 5:00. Patience was a virtue I definitely possessed; it was the one trait that made me good at my chosen professions.

A good hour and five false alarms later, Coulier eventually exited the building into the chill morning air.

She worked in the craft shop section of 'Banner's Garden Centre' on the farthest side of town, and being a fucking obnoxious do-gooder, who constantly felt the need to obviate her desires to save the planet, she would often opt to make the fairly extensive journey on foot. Except on Mondays of course, after her usual weekend of excessive drinking. Throwing up in the streets—I guess—to honour the beautiful world she apparently respected so very much.

She crossed the carpark and stopped, then looked across at her car.

I stiffened in my seat. "No! Don't you dare drive, bitch!" I said out loud.

I could see she was contemplating correcting her shitty parking, but if she got in the car and started the engine, I felt certain she'd end up driving to work, and that would majorly fuck with my plans.

Eventually though, she seemed to think better of it and left through the gate— inconsiderate moron that she was.

I rose from the car and quietly nudged the door shut with my hip. Then with my hood pulled up and pockets laden with everything I'd need—I set off to shadow her journey.

It was the final days of July and the early mornings were beginning to grow cold.

I tracked Coulier through the old-world beauty of Bradlington's chocolate box town centre.

Seventeenth century sandstone shops and cottages lined the old high street, and I often thought any traveling American would probably die of a quaint-induced coronary if they were to happen upon the place by accident.

The garden centre was on the opposite side of town, and Jennifer would take a well-trodden path across an area of land the locals called 'The Priest's Fields'.

It crossed from a timber-posted gateway off the end of Station Road and meandered over farmland to Aspley Church—ironically—the very place I'd secured the coffin nails the night before.

Could that be another sign? The lords of the underworld seemed to be choring their consent.

I made sure to keep as good distance back. The risk I was taking was enormous. If she 'were' to see me, how on earth would I explain my presence there, following her—both of us knowing full well that it was she who fuelled Marianna's suspicions. Suspicions that ultimately lead to her leaving me. I'd have to kill her—there and then—and that didn't fit in with my plans. So, back I hung.

I continued following, sighting every recessed doorway and alleyway entrance I might need to dive for, were she to suddenly stop and turn to look behind her.

Her chilled breath rolled over her huddled shoulders and dissolved into the slipstream of her hurried walk.

She had on a long, black coat and trendy, workmen-style boots. She used to dress like a doily goth, every spare flap of skin peppered with some form of decorative shrapnel to display to the world how quirky and out there she was.

I hated her—she tweaked my nerves—which was a shame, as beneath all of that over-thought, pretentious crap, Jennifer Coulier was actually an incredibly beautiful girl.

Eventually, she passed through the gates at the end of Station Road and made her way along the well-trodden footpaths that circled the perimeter of the field.

I could see she had headphones on and was immersed in her own little world—perfect.

I sped up slightly to move in closer and locked my eyes on her feet.

The ground was damp from an unusually heavy dew, ripe for leaving a clean footprint—even more luck.

Coulier eventually reached the farthest side of the first field.

She gathered her heavy skirts up around her knees and clambered over the stile in the corner beneath a large beech tree.

The ground there looked reasonably soft; the soil massaged to a buttery consistency from the unusually heavy footfall of the day-walkers that the summer months invariably brought to the countryside.

She was still unaware of my presence, so I quickly stepped aside into some bushes and lifted my gaze from beneath my hood.

I made a mental note of the tread pattern of her boots as she straddled the gateway, then carefully watched where she landed when she dropped off the other side.

She stumbled sideways as she landed, regained her balance, then set off again for the opposite corner of the next field.

With the pattern of her boots still fresh in my mind, I quickly ran across to the timber gate.

I arrived and leant over the top rail. The wood of the fencing had been warped by time and polished smooth by a thousand hands over a hundred years.

I could see where Jennifer had stumbled and had left for me a perfect imprint of her foot in the doughy earth.

I waited until she'd finished crossing the second field and was sure she was out of sight. Then straddled the stile and dropped onto the other side.

I crouched at the footprint, taking a quick look around to check I was alone.

I was, there were no witnesses present.

I carefully drew out the sheet of illustrated parchment from the large pocket of my hoodie and gently lay it in the footprint.

I pinned it in place with three of the coffin nails, then—with an image of my desires playing clearly in my mind like a movie—I raised a cone of power and said 'the words'.

The atmosphere around me changed, growing treacle-thick and pregnant with dread. I could sense the gates had opened, and 'he' was out.

Aishma had been summoned. He was loose and coming to do my bidding, and when he had, he would be visiting to collect yet another piece of me as payment for his services.

It was done. The curse was set. I rose and began scanning the field for stones.

Chapter Three

The Taking of Jennifer Coulier

FOR JENNIFER COULIER, the day in the craft shop had passed as an unusually quiet one. Wednesdays—for whatever reason—she usually found to be busy.

Maybe crafters had a tendency to run out of stock mid-week, and inexplicably, didn't seem to have jobs to go to. But whatever the reason—for her—that particular Wednesday had been untypically slow.

She bid her work colleagues 'goodbye', knowing little of the grim poignancy her words were to attain.

She made her way along the corridors of spades, hoes and forks of the tools section, throwing a wave to the entrance to the cafe and passing through the main tills.

Margret and Cherry were still cashing up, their mouths miming the figures each had taken.

Jennifer also bade them a good night, then erroneously called back, "I'll see you two tomorrow," over her shoulder, as she wafted an arm at the motion detector above the doors.

The small black box clicked, the light turned red, and with a turbine swish, the doors parted.

The relative freshness of the evening breeze shrunk back from an eruption of sun-warmed air escaping the glass building, and Jennifer Coulier stepped from the safety of the light into the flat stillness of dusk.

She traversed the fields. The air grew cold.

A cloudless sky, heavy with dusk, hung open above her skyward gazes, inviting the heat of the day to pass and dissipate into the cooling embrace of the stratosphere.

She drew a scarf from her pocket and wrapped it around her delicate neck, pulling the collar of her coat up high and burying her slender hands deep into her fur-lined pockets.

She crossed the Priest's Fields. Her tired eyes—thirsting from a day of confinement—drank in the splendour of the vistal views spread out before her.

The cool air chilled the walls of her nostrils as she breathed it in, her journey serenaded by the chattering barks of the jackdaws as they swooped in from the surrounding field maples to begin their search for food.

She arrived at the stile, stopped and turned a curious eye to the ground.

She stepped forwards and leaned in to examine a strange pyramid of stones that she felt almost certain weren't there eleven hours earlier.

Her brows flickered, and she presented the toe of her boot to the peculiar arrangement.

An image of the 'Stone Henge' that graces Salisbu ry's plains flashed into her mind. She considered the sanctity of the neolithic structure and withdrew the boot.

She would respect the stones and the will of whoever it was that had taken time and effort to arrange them. But that did nothing to quench her interest in why they were there and who had set them.

She backed away, turned and climbed the decrepit stile—hovering momentarily to dart her fermenting curiosity back at the stack of rocks. Then—lifting her trailing leg over—dropped onto the other side.

She crossed the open field towards the Station Road alleyway, chin buried deep in the warmth of her scarf, watching her legs kicking at the heavy hemline of her shin-length coat.

A sudden notion she was being watched and was anything but alone came over her, pulling her abruptly from her daydreams.

Her flitting eyes scanned the field before her, but she could see no one, only a light, vortexing plume of dust twisting from the far side of the land and across the scrubbed earth towards her.

Her eyes watched as it meandered across the sun-baked soil, lifting clipped blades of straw and dead leaves skyward as it tracked left, then right but always seemingly in her direction, until, it was only feet from where she was standing.

She took a few steps back, away from its strange, churning, localised motion, as it changed direction one last time and began moving directly towards her.

Jennifer's spine stiffened, stumbling backwards, holding a hand out towards it in attempt to halt its approach.

And then—it stopped, seeming to die in the air that had carried it to her, its curling tendrils melting away into the breeze like salt crystals in water, until once again, all was still.

The particles of dust dropped from the air like rain, and she breathed again. "What the fuck?" she muttered into the silence.

Jennifer felt the moist warmth of a soft breath part her jet-black hair and play up her neck.

She stiffened, sucked in air and spun around, lifting a hand to the bristling hairs on the nape of her neck.

A chilled feeling of violation sank through her feet. "Hello?" she called into the skein of light fog now blanketing the field, her voice unsteady. "Is there someone there?"

She hung in the unwelcoming disquiet of the wide-open space, listening to the urgent reciprocation of her own breaths.

The barks of the Jackdaws had ceased, and they were nowhere to be seen. She was alone but didn't feel it.

She gulped back her nerves. Her gloss-black lips grew dry. She licked them wet again and tentatively turned to continue across the field.

Her shoulders felt weighty, like she'd had a day of heavy lifting—which she hadn't.

She shrugged a few times to stretch away the tightness—but it remained.

She carried the heaviness home with her, confused fingers feeling at the thick hemline of her blanket coat, imagining it must somehow be waterlogged. But it wasn't, she frowned…

She finally arrived at her apartment block, swung the gate open and made her way across the parking lot.

She drew her keys from her pocket, shrugging at the leaden feeling in her yolk. She recalled there was an Osteopath on Forge Bank Lane. *Maybe I need to pay him a visit*, she thought to herself.

"Jenniferrrrrrrrrr," whispered a voice—breathy, taunting, from right behind her ear.

She barked a yelping scream and spun around.

The streetlights glowed with a tangerine warmth, but the air felt frigid. "Wh-Who is that?" she called—her widened eyes peering into the fog-heavy night-sky.

41

She cupped the violated ear in her cold hand, darted a look back at the right hand flowerbed and began to back slowly away from the feeling she was still being watched.

Her panicked fingers stuttered the key at the lock of the door, glancing worried eyes back over her shoulder.

The key finally juddered through the slot, the tumblers turned, and she hurried inside.

The automatic lobby lights flashed on, and she slammed the door shut behind her. The crash echoed up the marble-clad stairwell, then dissipated into total silence.

She spun around and pressed her face against the glass. She could see nothing. She shrugged again.

Jennifer turned from the door into the lobby. An 'Out of Order' sign adorned the elevator doors, alongside the mess of glue residue patches that shadowed the many times the lift had been out of service of late.

"Fucking maintenance," she muttered under her breath—her words echoing off the walls.

She made her way up the staircase, chased by a feeling of unease.

She stepped onto the landing and eyed the door to her apartment, briefly leaning over the handrail to take in the birds-eye view of the entrance hallway.

The motion-activated lights began shutting off one at a time, carrying a ring of darkness up the stairwell towards her.

She wheeled her hands in the air to make certain the lights to her floor remained on, then strode urgently to her apartment door.

She rolled her shoulders again, thrust the key into the lock, turned it, kneed the door open and rushed inside.

The door slammed shut, and she slumped her back against it.

She took in a slow, full breath to calm the quiver in her gut, then called to her friend. "Marianna?" she queried—softly, but her call was met with silence.

She stepped from the door, dropped her keys on the side table and swung her face into the living room. "Marianna?" she called, again—still nothing.

She pondered where her friend might be—her expectations for her to already be there proving fruitless.

She entered the kitchen. There was a handwritten note leant against the toaster on the kitchen island.

She took it up in her ring-encrusted fingers to read it—

Hi, Jen. I've just popped out to see Kirsty. I shouldn't be too long, but please, don't wait for me, just eat if you're hungry. I hope you had a good day at work… I'll see you soon. Love you. Mari xxx

Jennifer smiled—finally beginning to enjoy the feeling of having company around the flat—until then, she'd always lived alone.

She placed the note fondly back down against the toaster and moved into the hall unbuttoning her coat.

She stepped in front of her full length mirror, dropping her chin to her chest—shrugging the weighty garment back off her work-tired shoulders—then stepped to the side to hang it up.

Her cheeks winced as she flexed her neck, lifting her eyes to check herself in the reflection.

A fluid warmth trickled down her inner-thighs, as hot-amber rain poured from the laced hemline of her skirt, splashing off the hardwood flooring beneath her.

Her quivering top lip curled hard against her flaring nostrils, widened with fear.

She froze to stone as she peered into her reflection.

A dark, squat, impish figure sat crouched on her shoulders, barely visible in the shadows of the hallway, grinning its evil intentions from a face effervescent with mischief.

Her body began to shudder, but she couldn't move, petrified by the sight of the thing peering at her from within the gloom of the long room.

The entity's clawed feet gripped her shoulders, as it twisted its slouching body down, wrapping its spidery fingers around her scarf. But she could only see its arm reflected in the mirror, as its spindly hand passed her face.

The thing's absent grin turned skyward, and it reached up to grasp a run of exposed pipework projecting from above the door of the bathroom.

The godless entity threaded the scarf over the paint-encrusted pipes, gripped the wall with its wiry limbs and pulled.

Jennifer's entire bodyweight lifted from the balls of her feet, her delicate neck stretching long, panicked toes reaching desperately for the floor.

She kicked—feet slamming the walls as she lifted towards the ceiling.

The soft threads of wool pulled thin to string, cutting into her soft skin like cheese-wire.

Slender fingers clawed frantically at her tightening throat, friction burning her pale skin.

A tennis ball tongue flashed purple and began to push from her mouth. Her vision blurred to soft focus, claustrophobic neck chocking vain, stifled attempts to draw a breath.

The whites of her eyes ruptured blood-red—foam boiling from the sides of her distended tongue.

The entity heaved its twisted limbs to hoist her higher, its sharp teeth chattering its cruel pleasure.

She flailed violently, pirouette feet swiping helplessly for the feeling of floor, or the hallway chair, but in her vain attempts to reach it—kicked it over.

Her ruby-red, swollen eyes rolled independently in her 'why me?' expression, and with a final hysterical flurry of violently banging limbs, she fell limp and sagged to a lifeless ribbon.

The demon leaned out from the wall and drew its face level with Jennifer's swinging, bloated features.

It twisted its wicked smile, examining the results of its calling.

It pushed into her and inhaled the final gurgling breath seeping from her inert body.

The 'thing' extended an arid tongue from a mouth quivering with rapture and licked the froth from the corner off her blue-black lips, its drawn, grotesque body shaking with impure enjoyment at the taste of terror and confusion lacing the fear-formed excreter. Then it turned, crawled from the hallway and made its way along the ceiling of the living room.

It extended a pin-sharp finger down, flicked the latch off the window and slithered out into the cold, lightless night.

The task was done, the piper needed paying, and it set off through the slow, rolling mists to claim its pound of flesh.

Chapter Four

An Old 'Friend' Comes Visiting

I SPENT a majority of that day crafting the new poppet of Marianna, and as I neared completion of the doll, I felt sure night must have fallen.

My cellar workshop would attain a distinct type of chill when the sunlight left the soil, and the temperature had dropped noticeably, by a good five degrees.

My thumb flicked the switch of my angle poise and I peered up between the floorboards. But I could see no light from the kitchen, so I knew it must be dark outside.

Then I heard a noise behind me, a slow, hissing, hollow breathing sound emanating from somewhere within the darkness. It was a slow, hissing, hollow breathing sound I'd encountered before, but that did nothing to reassure me, only fill me with dread.

My insides sank like the Titanic, and I tried wishing it away. But the lengths I'd gone to, and the rituals I'd had to employ to bring this 'thing' into my world, were far too powerful to be reversed by any simple declaration of my desires, however strong they may have been.

I fumbled at the cable of my lamp, attempting to find the switch.

I could hear the breathing begin to move towards me, crawling along the wall on my left shoulder.

My stuttering fingers finally found the button, but I resisted pressing it and having to come face-to-face with the twisted entity that had materialised in the cellar with me.

I heard the clawing sound leave the wall and begin moving along my table towards me. He'd arrived, come for his piece of me in payment for his deeds.

The fact that he was there meant Jennifer Coulier must already have been dead, but I was far too afraid to feel pleased.

A deep 'thrum' emanated from my phone; I'd forgotten I'd taken it down there with me.

The screen flashed on, under-lighting an evil face grinning with malice, hovering barely an inch from my own.

I flinched; my breathing quickened. I tried to pull back from the distant look of cruelty in its black, marble eyes, but it just moved further into me.

My phone continued to 'hum'—vibrations spinning it on the worktop—flashing a name and number I daren't look away to see.

The demon crouched on the bench before me. My breaths became short and panting, burning the dryness in the back of my throat.

He leaned in and sniffed at my mouth, smelling the acidic fear colouring my breath, a fear that existed despite it being me who was foolish enough to summon him.

A clattering sound like striking hollow timbers emanated from behind its hunched shoulders. I could just make out—in the faint glow of the under-light—the heads of a ram and a bull projecting from its skeletal back, their horns clashing as they writhed expectantly.

He pushed further into me, lining his mouth up with mine and inhaled.

My whole inner self shifted and began pulling towards my throat.

I could feel my aura receding from my fingers, like I was being emptied. They tingled, then numbed. So did my feet.

My vision began to blur, as he sucked at my soul. It poured from my open mouth and clouded my face.

I fought to stay connected, trying in vain to draw myself back inside. That euphoric, impish demon imbibed me into his dry, powdery lungs. The clattering of the horns grew more frantic with every suck at my waning vitality.

It bit down with its sharded teeth, swallowed and released what little remained, and with a jarring 'thud', I re-entered myself.

Tears ran the gauntlet of my trembling cheeks. He had claimed much of me, way more than he had ever taken before. A life force vampire feeding off my ill intent and resentment.

My shaking thumb still hovered over the switch as the tide of my depleted soul flowed slowly back through my body and into my fingertips.

The feeling in my hands returned, and I clicked on the lamp, just in time to watch the crooked entity passing back into 'his' world, melting away through the shadows in the un-lit corner of my cellar workshop.

And as quickly as he had come, he was gone again.

My entire ashen face crumpled, and tears streamed from my eyes.

I huffed whimpering sobs for my humbled vulnerability, and I knew it would be a long, long time before I would dare summon any such entity again.

It suddenly dawned on me that it had been eighteen years since I last raised Aishma, when Marianna's over-zealous, interfering mother needed removing from the picture.

I sat slouched, weeping, until my tears dried into thick films of salty regret coating my entire face. Not regret for my actions, only for my poorly chosen method of execution.

I stretched my face long to pull myself from the moment. I felt the dried tears splitting on my cheeks, and then I remembered—someone had been trying to call me.

I took up the phone in my shaking hands and stuttered my thumb at the screen. I strained my smudged vision to read the name.

My empty heart sang out. I gazed at the phone like a child with a gift at Christmas. The call—it was from Marianna.

I erupted into what little life remained at the sight of her name. An image of her perfect features and supermodel smile flashed into my lonely mind. Then I noticed the 'voicemail' symbol pulsing in the top right-hand corner of the screen. In my eagerness, I tapped it.

A calm voice drifted in from the earpiece. "You have one new message. New messages." Then it beeped.

What followed was something as close to impossible to listen to as anything could ever be. I was faced with a three-minute, twenty-four-second torturous cacophony of bawling, wailing, distraught and hopeless screaming. Inconsolable tears and desperate, lamenting, choking grief.

I pulled the phone from my ear, guilt briefly manifesting in my gut. I took a full breath and exhaled it away.

I raised the phone midway to my ear again. "Samualllll, oh God, she's dead! Jennifer's dead. Oh God, noooooooo. No, no, no, no, no—" she wept.

Guilt visited me again. "No. Fuck off! Fuck her!" I spat—dropping the phone from my ear again. "Fucking Coulier, she had it coming," I seethed—attempting to fight regret's attempts to birth in my conscience.

I jabbed my finger at the screen to stop the harrowing sound and sat uneasily in my thoughts and actions for a time.

Then my mind began to work again as it should, figuring out ways to make use of Marianna's grief.

'Observe, Learn, Apply'—my mantra for life. It had stood me in good stead for the previous twenty-five years, and that was definitely something, in light of the task that lay ahead of me, that I needed to remember.

I gathered up in my tattered resolve. I had to remain strong if I was to win back my ideal life. An ideal life that the interference of those meddling 'bitches' had taken from me.

I rose to the kitchen and made some camomile tea to calm the feeling I'd been violated. Which I had.

I carried it to the table, sat with my phone and gently dabbed my finger on Marianna's number. It began to ring…I took a sip of the tea.

Someone answered. "Marianna?" I said, my voice urgent. "It's Sam, are you okay? What the hell's happened?" I asked in the most knowledge-less, kind and querying voice I could muster.

"Oh God, Sam, nooooo," she bawled, "it's Jennifer. Jennifer's gone. She's gone, oh God, oh God, oh God, oh God, oh God—" she cried, the pleas to her Lord morphing to inconsolable, sobbing tears. Tears to a supposed 'God' that failed to appear and spare Jennifer's pointless existence.

"What do you mean, 'Gone'?" I asked—curious to know exactly what the demon I'd called upon had done. The confusion I wove into my voice could have bagged an Oscar.

"Shhhhhhe killed herself."

"What?" I said—in feigned, shocked disbelief. "How?"

She choked through her words—"I found her, hanging. When I got back, I found herrrrrrr. She'd. She'd. Oh no please, this can't be happening, pleeeeease—"

I sat quietly on the end of the phone—because that's what you would do if you were genuinely shocked. But in reality, hearing what 'He' had done, the pretence wasn't at all necessary—I 'was' shocked.

"But—why?" I eventually asked. "I can't believe it," I added. Convincing? I thought so.

She broke down and began gagging through her grief. I started to feel her pain again, and that was dangerous.

"Listen. Marianna, you still have some clothes here, just come back, even if it's just for tonight, you really shouldn't be alone. I-I can sleep in the spare room if you'd prefer. But please, just come home—okay, I'm so sorry."

Then I realised, I had sounded far too desperate, far too insistent, and I knew it. Too much too soon, but it was too late to unsay my words.

She suddenly went silent on me, save for the occasional sniffle and stuttered intake of breath.

I could hear her thinking about what I'd said. "Oh Sam. That's really nice of you, but—I'm." She paused. "I'll be staying with Kirsty tonight; she's here with me now," she said.

I pulled the phone from my ear and began grinding the blades of my teeth to dust. I was livid.

That other stain on my life—Kirsty fucking Green and her 'friend-to-all', 'always-there-for-you', interfering bitch ways.

Friend to all—but not to me. Another obstacle that needed to be removed.

But I couldn't just kill her—not this one—that would raise far too many suspicions.

She'd have to be eradicated, pushed aside, to clear the pathway to my happiness.

I knew what I had to do. It would take more work, more effort, more risk, but Marianna, my dearest, darling Marianna, she was sure as hell worth it.

My anger had given me back my resolve. I feigned understanding to show her just how nice I could be and told her—I would always be there for her, come what may.

Then I rang off, to begin the next steps of my 'project'.

I descended into my workshop again—giving a cautious look around to check Aishma wasn't there, waiting for me.

If I'm to be perfectly honest, I never truly trusted him. I often felt like, that in 'me' raising 'him', it somehow always ended up being on 'his' terms.

But he, 'it', was nowhere to be seen. I breathed a deep sigh of relief to clear my knotted stomach. "Okay," I said out loud to re-focus my mind. I was shaking.

I'd had an idea earlier that day about a new 'life-box'. But this time, it would be hidden, not just locked.

I figured—a location that's secret would be far safer than one that's just suspiciously inaccessible. So I decided that's what I would do.

It only took me about two hours of work to complete it; I was always good with my hands.

I was one of those people who could turn his creativity to just about anything he cared to, so constructing a hidden draw that slid beneath my entire materials cabinet was a cinch.

I screwed in the last two fixings, then walked back and crouched to check you couldn't see it. You couldn't, it was invisible—perfect!

I glanced down at the deconstructed marionette lying on the end of my bench, it needed finishing and handing over.

Its incompletion taunted me. Lying there, undone, in pieces—just like my life.

But as long as that Kirsty Green stood in the way of the path back to happiness, I knew I'd struggle to ever give a shit enough to finish it, and I found myself more than willing to make the client wait. I had far more important things to do that day.

With the new poppet of Marianna in hand—I climbed the ladder that rose into the loft space of the cottage.

It was a dry, draughty, dust-laden space, decorated with long sweeps of cobweb bunting that drifted gently in the warm air rising from the open hatch.

I switched on the single bulb that hung from the gable, illuminating a block of sandstone sitting directly beneath it.

The ironically named cellar-spiders fumbled ungracefully back from the light, into the safety of the shadows that the insipid light source created.

It was in this very space—at the very top of the house—where you would find my ceremonial circle.

Marianna had always harboured an acute fear of insects, especially spiders, so neither hell nor high water could ever convince her to go up into a space such as that. So that particular secret remained safe and made the spiders watching me from the rafters my friends.

I carefully stepped inside a thick, encrusted ring of salt that encircled the entire area. It was within that circle of protection that I performed my rituals.

I laid the doll down on the altar, drew a match from its box and struck it.

The stick fizzed into life, and I presented the rolling flame to the wick of a heavy, black candle rising like an obelisk from the centre off the stone.

The slow dancing flame leaped across to the tip of the string. It flickered weakly, fighting to stay alight, then caught, swelled and climbed down the wax-soaked chord—its brightness intensifying until the old beams of the loft space glowed amber.

The spiders watched me work from within their webs. A thousand eyes in groups of eight, reflecting the candle flame back at me.

In my earlier days practising Witchcraft, I would wear robes. Just one part of a fixed routine that helped set my mind in the right frame, breaking me free of the crippling normality of the everyday world, to help me descend into the darker corners of my psyche. A place you need to learn to feel comfortable in to be successful.

But as time passed, and my skills became more second nature, I found I could dispense with the cloak and other extraneous parts of my rituals.

I knelt before the altar, the smell of the sulphur from the struck match hanging in the air and carefully drew three rose petals I'd secured from the garden from my pocket and threaded them onto a pin.

I pressed it into the poppet of Marianna, through the area of her heart.

My fingers carefully positioned a passport picture of me face-down against that of the doll, then threaded two more pins carefully through the eyes of the photo and into the eyes of the poppet.

I made peace with my thoughts, attained an inner calm few have ever experienced, then leant in and whispered into the ear of the effigy.

I spoke to it of many thing: what it was, who it represented and that it was I, and only I, that was to be master of its destiny.

I raised another cone of power. It hung churning in the air above the altar, burning as bright as any sun, and with a sweep of the hands and a thrust of my wants, I projected it out from the house—binding the energies of the poppet to Marianna—and just like that, it was done.

I carefully lifted the poppet from the stone. I was almost certain I felt it twitch in my hands. The shock nearly made me drop it from my fingers.

I wasn't sure if it was the heightened levels of need and ultimate longing I was feeling when I'd crafted it, or simply how much I was missing the sensual touch of that incredible woman when I linked the effigy to 'her'.

But whatever the reason, this thing was fizzing with life, the exact same fizz I would feel through my fingertips whenever I touched Marianna. And that's how I knew my work was good.

Now all I needed was an effigy of Kirsty Green to complete the trinity: one of her, the one of me, and the doll of my beloved Mari that lay in my adoring hands, and with those three things, and the calm, tranquil patience of a saint—I could move worlds.

I knew where Kirsty worked. I knew the time she knocked off. And I had a plan.

Chapter Five

The Binding of Kirsty Green

THE 'GREEN' GIRL OWNED A GIFT SHOP. One of those godforsaken places one would frequent if you wished to purchase a fatuous present without the need to expend any real thought or heartfelt consideration.

Choose it. Buy it. Drop in a gift bag and pass it across a hastily booked table at some emotionless, trendy chain restaurant to honour your oh-so-valued friendship to that particular evening's forgettable centre of attention, sat in a self-absorbed importance amidst a circle of likeminded, shallow friendships.

I'd always struggled to not laugh whenever we 'popped in', 'just to say 'hi''. To not fold double and piss myself with laughter at the ridiculous mix of inane, meaningless, trite and pretentious garbage that peppered the rustic shelving and hung from the exposed beams.

A shop filled to the rafters with all manner of junk that no one could possibly ever need: papier-mâché hot air balloons carrying cutesy teddy-bears. Resin figurines of weeping children holding signs that say 'I Wuv You', or 'Hug Me'. Volkswagen Beetles made of tin. Laurel and Hardy bookends made of low-grade plaster. Gaudy dragons made of faux-ceramic plastics and shelf upon shelf of signs saying 'HOUSEWIVES DRINK GIN', or 'COME ON, GIRLS, IT'S WINE O'CLOCK'. Shit. Shit. Shit. A pompous shop for morons filled to the brim with meaningless shit.

But people went in there. People bought things. And in a market economy, it's hard to argue with the numbers.

But to me, it stood as a shining testament in shop-form to the sheer, unadulterated lack of imagination of the public as a whole. A shrine to people's unwillingness to make any real effort to show how they truly feel about each other. To fail to give meaningfully, so that down the line, they may receive something of value in return.

But instead, they choose to swap shit for shit. Meaningless gesture for meaningless gesture.

Yet another turd fouling the high streets of this beautiful country. 'Observe, Learn, Apply.'

My plan was to orchestrate a chance meeting with Kirsty as she locked up the shop for the night. A 'happened to be passing this way' accident.

I dressed up smart. Casual—but smart.

I was under no illusion that in contriving Marianna into my life, I was punching well above my barely measurable weight—as the saying goes.

But if I made the effort, if I 'actually' tried, I could make a reasonable fist of not looking to out of place standing next to someone as ethereally statuesque and criminally beautiful as my Marianna was, and that was something I wanted Kirsty Green to see.

She usually shut up shop at around 5:30 and be out of the door by 5:45.

I hung outside of the estate agents on the corner by the townhall, pretending to look at the come-and-buy-me property listings that tiled the windows.

I heard the door to the shop open, and Kirsty stepped out into the soft, evening light.

She was wearing a light-weight coat and had a large tote bag hooked over her shoulder.

She turned to lock the door, and I set off—hands in my pockets, eyes to the ground, as though in my own little world.

I peered from beneath my brows and headed straight towards her. She turned from the door and stuttered when she saw me.

I lifted my eyes to meet hers. "Oh. Kirsty. Hi," I said, with warm surprise.

"Oh—h-hey, Sam," she responded—awkwardly.

She looked thoroughly uncomfortable to see me there, and I could tell she'd rather have been anywhere else.

I saddened my brows, sagged my shoulders a little and winced one of those weak, understanding smiles.

"I heard about Jennifer, isn't it awful?" I said. She replicated my face and nodded. "How are you coping?" I asked with a tilt of my head. "Are you okay?"

She flinched an anorexic smile and nodded. "Yeah, I-I'm doing all right. But it's not easy, is it? It's just really sad, a-and tragic," she muttered.

"I know," I responded—lowering my eyes. "I just can't—" I loosed a sighed. "I just never knew, or, or ever thought she felt that way, or-or would do anything like that," I said.

Kirsty's eyes began to moisten—something I could make use of. "Ohhh God, I'm sorry. I'm so sorry," I mewed. "Let's not talk about it, okay?"

She nodded and crimped an appreciative smile.

I flashed understanding eyes. "Is, em, is Marianna coping okay?" I asked. "And, don't worry," I added, "I'm giving her the space she wants; I'd just like to know if she's okay. I can't help caring about her."

Kirsty nodded and smiled kindly. "Yes, she's doing okay; she's fine."

I smiled back at her. "Good," I whispered.

I hung in the cloud of sadness that hovered between us. Hers genuine, mine faked. "Would you please just say 'hello' for me when you see her, and let her know I'm thinking about her. *Would* you do that for me?"

She agreed—seemingly happily. But I couldn't quite work out if she meant it or not. "Okay. I'll certainly do that for you. No problem," she said.

I smiled back at her. "Thank you, Kirsty, I really appreciate that," I said with sincerity.

I lifted my hands from my pockets and stepped forwards to give her a hug. She stiffened slightly in my arms, then seemed to allow herself to relax into my display of kindness.

She dropped her bag onto the ground and put her arms around me. "I do love her, you know," I said, my words true.

She hung in my declaration for a few seconds. "I know. I know," she replied, in whispered tones.

I loosed the embrace and stepped back again, putting my hands back in my pockets and shrugging a parting smile. "Well, take care of yourself, Kirsty," I said, softly.

"Yeah. And you, Sam."

I never realised until that moment just how likeable and attractive Kirsty Green could actually be. Her smile was kind and her eyes bright. And the gloss of her brunette hair caught the rays of the sinking sun and glowed chestnut brown.

Birds of a feather, I guess. But when I think about it, all of Marianna's friends were in some way beautiful. Like attracts like, except I existed as the glaring exception that shattered that rule. Like a dirty smut on the pure whiteness of an angel's wing.

We parted and went our separate ways, and I made my way back to the car.

I'd parked up on Hope Street, just outside of the town's small, independent cinema.

It was a wonderfully quaint little place, styled to be evocative of hay-day of cinema. A faded glamour to its forties' Hollywood decor.

Every few months, they'd run seasons of specific genres of movie: Sci-Fi. Horror. Film noir. Romance. Musicals. Comedy, you name it—something for everyone.

It was a favourite haunt of mine and Marianna's, before she searched out my box, and it all went to shit. I longed to win those times back again.

I unlocked the door of the car, climbed inside and started the engine.

I took a look around to check I was clear of prying eyes, straightened my body in the seat and slid my hands into my pockets.

I pulled out a pair of scissors, a lock of brown hair and a slice of Kirsty's scarf and carefully dropped them into a zip-lock bag on the passenger seat and sealed it.

I now had everything I needed to set the hex.

I was already in possession of her personal details—they were logged in my book of shadows back at the house, along with those of everyone else in Marianna's close circle of friends: their full names. Dates of birth. Hours of birth. Star signs. Heights. Weights. Likes. Dislikes and all their defining personality traits.

Snippets of information gathered over time under the guise of meaningless conversation and polite banter, listed in my little black book in case of need and one of those needs had arisen.

I arrived back at the cottage and set to work immediately, toiling through the night and not stopping for anything until my task was complete.

At gone midnight, I climbed down from the loft holding the newly bound effigy of Kirsty in my hands.

I hovered at the base of the steps in the brighter light of the landing to consider my work.

I felt weirdly pleased I wasn't to kill this one, having actually found myself liking Kirsty earlier that day.

She was genuine and nice to me, and in reality—by her actions—she was just being a good friend to my Marianna.

But ultimately, when all's said and done, she 'was' still stood in the way of my desires, my happiness, so would have to be moved aside.

I dropped into the familiar comfort of my cellar workshop again, the place—more than any other on the planet—I'd spent a vast majority of my life.

I knelt down in front of my materials cabinet and pulled out my newly constructed, secret drawer.

I stretched up and grabbed the poppets off my work-bench and began arranging them in the virgin 'life-box'.

The poppet of me—that was placed in the far left-hand side of the drawer, the one of Kirsty—to the far-right.

I looked down into my hands, down at the poppet of my dearest, beautiful Marianna and stared fondly at it lying in the caress of my fingertips.

I lifted it to my nose and sniffed at the hair I'd painstakingly knotted onto its head. Each strand still smelled of her—a sweet-scented earthiness.

For the first time in days, I felt calm, a stillness to my solitude, an inner peace at the knowledge that soon, the tumbling honey-blonde hair, the sensuous, deep-red, glossed lips, the sky and royal-blue flecked Egyptian eyes, the straight, ballerina-backed perfection of her sublimely seductive spine, and the legs, the mile-long perfection of those cat-walk legs that could arrest a heartbeat and cease a breath would all soon be back in my life again. Back with me—there to stay.

I placed the gentlest of kisses onto the forehead of the doll and laid it carefully next to the one of Kirsty, and I was ready. The long, drawn-out ritual could finally begin.

The board had been set, and the first move would be made in the morning. The opening gambit in a weeklong game of chess that ultimately, I would win.

I slid the drawer back under and took to my bed for the remainder of the night.

All such things as these take time and great patience. The patience of a saint but the unsatisfiable hunger and unquenchable thirst of a devil.

The bed felt bleak and empty, but I slept sound in the company of the knowledge that things wouldn't be that way for very much longer.

I awoke the next day to empty skies. The night-time heavens had hung cloudless and star-filled, and the subsequent morning air had an arctic freshness that aided waking.

I stood leaning in the doorway that overlooked the patio with a strong mug of tea in hand to witness the unveiling of the day. The air felt strangely sanguine and optimistic.

A robin flitted in and perched in the conifer across the way from me and began to sing in my direction. A 'very' good omen indeed. A sign. A signifier. A message of impending good fortune, a reigniting of a lost passion and the rebirthing of some lost element of my life, and I knew at that very moment, all was to come good.

The bold little bird beeped, chirped and trilled for me for good ten minutes, warming the breeze with its vibrant song.

I thanked him with a handful of feed, and we both went our separate ways, to work to accomplish our very different agendas.

I felt settled and carried a second mug of tea down the flight of steps into the workshop, to finally complete the commission piece that had lay unfinished on the end of my table for far too long, and not forgetting—make that first move.

I sat down and drew the parts of the marionette into the centre of the bench before me and began to re-familiarise myself with where I was with the build.

I took a sip of my tea, the hot, rising steam fogging my vision as I peered over the rim of the mug, eyeing my materials cabinet.

I 'needed' to make that first move, but I was purposefully resisting to set a calm, patient tone to the processes.

But then I realised, I already felt calm, thanks mainly to the optimistic song of the robin and what that signified.

So I rose, rounded the end of my bench and sank to the flagstone floor.

I carefully drew out my secret drawer and peered down at the opening setup.

The initial moves in these things are inherently simple, but as the processes advance and evolve, they become far more intense.

The poppet of Marianna lay next to the effigy of Kirsty, their little cloth hands touching. A replication of the current situation to establish a solid link to the reality I was about to manipulate.

I closed my eyes and drowned my thoughts in my desires; my mind billowing with images of the way I wished things to be.

I reached into the drawer and moved Marianna's poppet slightly to the left— an inch away from Kirsty and an inch closer to me. And that was it, that's all I needed to do to open play.

I slid the draw back in gently so to not disturb the setup and rose to my feet again.

The next move would be made later that day.

I settled back at my bench and began the intricate task of finishing the marionette, a commission piece for a client in the Midlands.

I was one of only a handful of people on the sceptred isle that still undertook such work. An ancient artform, almost as ancient as the use of magic.

It could be said that both of my chosen crafts—but more importantly, 'witchcraft'—came from a forgotten time. A time when imaginations were far less stilted, and the eventual understanding of the sciences that explain much of our world hadn't created an ignorance in the population to erroneously dismisses the validity of something that has existed for as long as man itself.

But their dismissal gives my kind a place to exist. Their lack of belief leaves their kind weak and without guard, making it a pathetically simple proposition in these modern times to control their meaningless lives and steer their aimless destinies to one more in keeping with 'my' requirements.

When you think about it—the irony—it's deafening.

I lifted my eyes to the crescent of marionettes watching me work. An audience of misfits—like myself: A clown. A Jester. A matched pair of medieval princesses, one in blue chiffon, the other yellow. A dappled horse, a dog and the Hunchback of Notre Dame.

I could feel them all watching their creator, their 'God'—as it were. Working to finish the newest member of their species.

"What are you all looking at?" I said, as I toyed with the limbs of my puzzle. But as ever, they remained silent and just carried on watching with interest.

My eyes lifted further, to two more puppets hanging quietly at the back of the group.

I stood and reached over, unhooking them from their stands, lifting them over the fascinated throng and lowering them onto the table-top.

Each of my hands held a marionette. One of me and one of Marianna.

I'd fashioned them years earlier, when my love was still young and keen, and I remembered to be grateful for what I had, before allowing myself to become complacent about having the single most beautiful woman I'd ever laid eyes on sharing my life. My 'fantasy girl', holding me, kissing me, filling my desperate longing with her much dreamed-of care and attention.

My fingers hooked the strings, and I began to puppeteer our first kiss—a moment in my life I was never to forget. It marked my success. My reward. A monumental moment that I felt completed me.

Day became midday. Midday became night.

I finished stringing the marionette and carefully hooked it on a hanger to allow the final, finishing touches dry.

I stood and moved back to admire my work. An exquisitely crafted and meticulously detailed Pierrot hung before me. A far cry from my earliest work.

I made my first puppet when I was just nine years of age. No other word other than 'terrible', or perhaps 'deformed', could've been employed to describe this thing. But I remember feeling so proud of what I'd created.

It was then that I discovered I had a talent for puppeteering. A natural ability for controlling actions and reactions, and those talents for control would eventually prove useful in my later foray into witchcraft and the black-arts.

I tidied my bench and cleared the tools away. I was meticulous and painstakingly neat in the way I worked.

The chill had returned that hailed the fall of night, and I made my way around to the cabinet to make the next move.

My fingers fumbled beneath the large chest and pulled out the drawer. I leaned in—imagining Marianna's return and willing it real—then I moved her doll another inch, again, away from Kirsty and closer to me, then I slid the drawer back under.

A deep hum vibrated through the bench—I'd received a message.

I struggled to my feet and leant across to grab the phone from the bench and see who it was from. It was a text message—from Marianna.

I opened it.

'Hi, Sam, I hope you are well.

Kirsty said she saw you today. I'm just letting you know that the funeral for Jennifer is being held on Friday 23rd at 11:15 at the Holy Trinity Church if you wanted to go and pay your respects.

Maybe I'll see you there.

Take care of yourself.

Marianna. x

There was a second 'hum' and vibration. Another message landed.

P.S. I know we need to talk about things, but I just need a little more time. See you Friday, maybe. M. x

It was all I could do to not stare at the single, lower-case kiss glaring back at me. I could almost sense her hesitating, wondering whether to delete it or not.

But I paid it no mind; I knew it wouldn't be very much longer before she was ending all such messages with three, or maybe even five kisses. All caps and sent without second thought.

That first day had come to a close, nine more to go before my angel would be returning home to me.

The funeral was in just three days' time—mid-ritual—which was, or at least 'felt', inconvenient. But at least, it would gift me a chance to see her again and judge how well my life-path-adjustments were working—if at all.

I glanced at the Pierrot and then at the cabinet, then flicked off the lamp and rose from the chill of the cellar to prepare myself some well-earned dinner.

On each day leading up to the funeral, I patiently made my moves—inch, by inch, by inch. Gradually sliding Marianna away from Kirsty and closer to me.

Day three—I upped the ante. With every move of the doll, I began pouring a wall of salt along the growing divide between the poppets of Marianna and Kirsty. A crystalline barrier that would slowly extend between them, alienating their affections, splitting them apart. A creeping barricade that would work to weaken a lifelong friendship.

Day four finally arrived—the day of the funeral.

I possessed just one suit, charcoal grey—smart for meetings, light enough for weddings but dark enough to wear to a funeral.

I wasn't what you'd would call a 'suit kind of guy'. They felt awkward on me, unnatural and hung uncomfortably on my below-average frame.

I also loathed the feeling of constriction I had to endure when circumstance and convention forced the wearing of a tie, and I most certainly wasn't the type that could've ever held an office job.

My normal choice of clothing aired on the side of loose-fitting, allowing me a freedom to move, think and create.

I sure as hell couldn't begin to comprehend the innate ability females seemed to possess for wearing tightfitting clothing.

I would feel uncomfortable just seeing the pulled-tight creasing under their arms, or the concertina bunching around a stomach when a girl sat down.

Except with Mari though—that was different. Different in the same way that for most, that passing trend for hipster jeans that came, and thankfully went, made a mockery of the average female body—muffin-top obliques spilling over that ridiculously low waistband like Archimedes' bathwater.

But on a female-form of svelte proportions and sustained by a healthy diet and rigorous exercise, they could look incredible.

And it was the same thing with tightfitting clothing. Fine-fabrics stretched across firm, lithe bodies; I could never tire of that. And the queen of 'that' look—was Marianna.

I finished getting ready for the funeral, but I was running late.

I quickly jogged down into the cellar to move the poppet and pour the next inch of salt crystals.

The doll of Marianna was nearing the centre of the drawer, and I knew that soon, if not already, she would begin thinking of me with far greater frequency. Either in her thoughts, or her dreams but preferably both.

I gently lowered my suit-clad self into my car and started the engine.

The day that lay ahead promised to be hard-work; I would have to be on my best behaviour.

I harboured a hatred of churches and their pompous, money-grabbing ceremonies. But I would try my hardest to endure the day—if only for the greater good.

Chapter Six

Farewell to Thee, White Witch

IT ONLY OCCURRED TO ME on the journey there that this supposed celebration of the life of a devout Wiccan was being held at a church and not a woodland clearing in some idyllic, fairy-tale forest.

But then I remembered—she'd once told me at some gathering or other that her parents were staunch Christians, the type who would attend mass every Sunday without fail.

I thought—how typically Christian it was to blatantly ignore the will of their own daughter and on the occasion of her death. I couldn't help but laugh.

I arrived at the church. I had to admit, it was an impressively beautiful building. Comfortingly gothic and suitably awe-invoking in that way religious structures naturally contrive to be, to fool the masses into believing that awe to be the presence of some god. It was just a shame that it existed for all the wrong reasons.

I parked up and checked myself in the mirror. I looked smart but would have to make a concerted effort to not fidget inside the tailored discomfort of that fucking suit and resist rolling my neck and pecking my head in that cockney-gangster way at the unnatural tightness of the buttoned collar and tie.

I took a quick look in all of my mirrors; I was hungry for a glimpse of my Marianna. But she was nowhere to be seen.

I exited the car, forced a respectful gate and entered the church.

I smiled weakly and nodded at the minister who was hanging by the doors, the exact same way the people ahead of me had.

He smiled back at me with such faked sincerity that I had to fight hard to not laugh at the sheer hypocrisy of it all.

I shuffled in time with the rest of the mourners cuing towards the centre aisle, trying to spy a seat near the back where I could be inconspicuous and watch the proceedings with morbid interest.

I saw one, next to the rest of the stragglers who would also rather have been anywhere else and sat down.

Order of service pamphlets had been dealt onto the shelves before us. I took one up and flicked through it.

I sniggered, as not one of the photos of Coulier showed her in her Wiccan garb. I even fancied I saw a badly photoshopped area in one of the pictures where the amulet she always wore would have hung. Those fuckers had painted it out—hilarious. Christian assholes.

I felt a light, friendly tap on my shoulder and turned to see who delivered it.

I looked up and saw Marianna, her face back-lit by the sun streaming through the stained glass window behind her.

She flashed a kind, apologetic smile and mouthed the word 'hi'.

In the midst of the halo of the burning sun, she looked like an angel, a god, the mother of all things.

My perception of her infinite beauty had been reset by her absence and the passage of time, and I looked upon her again with the same souring levels of awe I felt the first time I ever saw her.

I could have wept at the feelings of joy infusing my body at seeing her face again.

I smiled a genuine smile. "Hi Mari," I whispered—my voice dripping with affection.

She smiled again below sad eyes, and her hand left my shoulder. "I'll talk to you later," she said through her blood-red lips.

I nodded, trying hard not to display the enthusiasm that was trying to breech my respectful facade, but it was impossible not to show it.

I watched her as she made her way up the aisle to the front row. She wore a long, black pencil skirt and a matching fitted jacket. My God, she looked graceful.

I leant out from the pew and lowered my gaze. Her long, slender legs rose elegantly from black, high-glossed heals, calves rippling as she strode.

I stirred and leaned forwards to hide it.

Her tumbling hair cascaded over the elegant slope of her shoulders, the shining contrast of silken honey-blonde on black illuminating the entire room, and she drew every male eye in the building, including mine.

She took a seat at the end of the pew, right next to the aisle.

I stretched up to see who it was she sat next to—it was Kirsty.

I watched them with an obvious interest to observe the hue of their interactions.

Mari leant over and whispered something. Kirsty cocked an ear and listened, then turned around and looked my way, her eyes scanning the back row until they settled on me.

I was looking straight at her which made her baulk slightly. But she styled it out by smiling, then mouthing, "Hey."

I smiled and nodded back at her. "Hey," I mimed in response. I widened my eyes sympathetically. "Are you okay?" I asked.

She indicated that she was, flashing kind eyes and turned back to the front.

There was a pause in their exchange. They both sat looking straight ahead to show me I wasn't being talked about. But they only managed to hold out for a matter of seconds before they were back, huddled together, swapping their views and opinions.

But the conversation between them seemed subtly strained? Marianna darting the occasional look in my direction mid-sentence.

I got a strong impression from the tone of their actions that Kirsty was trying to talk Mari out of her inexplicably softening feelings towards me, but her opinion only seemed to aggravate Marianna and fall on deaf ears.

I allowed myself a wry grin. If my observations were correct—if I 'was' reading them accurately—it meant things were working.

I looked around at the rest of the congregation. I knew roughly a quarter of the faces there, due mainly to my association with Marianna, but there were also a few faces I recognised from my school days.

Then I noticed—they all seemed to be glancing my way?

I suddenly realised—in focussing all of my attentions on the front row—I'd failed to notice I was sat at the core of a spreading buzz of gossip. And after a few minutes, there wasn't a single ear in the building that hadn't received, with interest, the news of mine and Marianna's relationship issues.

I flushed red. I hated being watched and even more than that, being talked about.

It reminded me of school, where anyone who cared to notice me would think me weird, or odd and used that most popular of opinions as ammunition for their ridicule.

71

Fuck them, I thought to myself. I cared little for their mocking opinions. The only opinion in that room that meant anything to me was sat on the front row and glancing back at me with increasing regularity.

If I was there for a reason, it was to show them all how wrong they all were about me, so I would be courteous—say hello when greeted. Smile when smiled to.

But in reality, I was there for one person and one real reason. And to my mind, the only human being who existed in my 'entire' realm of 'give-a-shit'— was Marianna.

Heads began spinning like meerkats. The coffin had arrived.

We all rose from our seats, and Jennifer's crated body was wheeled through the corridor of twisting looks and saddened eyes.

I mimicked their actions, wanting to blend in—Observe, Learn, Apply.

I felt weirdly powerful to be looking on as the orchestrator of her death. Feeling the way, I imagined a god would feel with the power that 'it' wields.

Was I a god? I wondered. I felt like one?

As the procession of bearers neared the front of the throng—the wailing started.

Her mother began to reach for the coffin and cry hysterically. At least, I presumed it was her mother, based on the unhinged levels of frenzied hysteria.

I'd seen her outside before we all went in. She had that holier-than-thou, better-than-you-are Christian look that forever rubbed me up the wrong way. A smiling facade to mask the superior contempt for others their kind truly feel inside.

Her brow-beaten husband worked respectfully to try to minimise the amount of 'fool' she made of herself. But her grieving set the rest of the room off, and before long, I was the only person there not shedding tears.

I felt an insatiable urge to stand on the seat and scream—"Pull yourselves together, you bunch of fucking morons." But instead, for the greater good, I joined in—if only in appearance.

I dropped my head into my cupped hands, dribbled saliva on the ends of my fingers and dabbed the wetness beneath my eyes.

I lifted my face again and began a routine of sniffling and exhaling distressed breaths.

I blended in beautifully—a grief-chameleon.

The priest mounted his lectern and began bleating his monotonous tripe: half eulogy. Half church sales pitch.

The congregation sank into a torporific state and listened blindly, without truly hearing anything of what was said, or understanding anything of what was happening: rising to their feet embarrassingly late each time a hymn had begun. Sitting again, hesitantly, only because they'd been instructed to.

The handful of church regulars obviated their superior knowledge of the way it all worked: Standing early, sitting early and kneeling when the time to blindly mumble yet another meaningless plea to a god that wasn't interested drew near.

But what fascinated me most, was that they all looked weirdly smug in their obviation of their willingness to comply—strange.

But Christ, I hated churches. The way those twats mindlessly said what they were told to say and sing what they were told to sing.

Going through motions without knowledge of what any of it actually meant. Following the rest of the clueless herd like the will-less sheep they were.

But what made me laugh loudest, and with unreserved freedom more than any of it, is that these places didn't even try to hide what was happening—'I am your shepherd, and you are my flock.'

They just said it out loud—as blatant as anything—and these morons were all too fucking stupid and brainwashed to even notice.

I almost respected the church for having the nerve and sheer audacity to take the piss so blatantly and so obviously—I said almost.

So I made a decision. I would focus all of my attention on my beloved Marianna to quell an impulse to laugh that had set up home in my diaphragm.

She looked incredible, and it warmed my heart each time she glanced back at me, smiling coyly over the recurved sweep of her elegant shoulder.

During the endless number of prayers that seemed to pepper the hourlong marathon of forced sincerity, I closed my eyes and imagined holding her again. Feeling her breathe next to me as I hung in the scent of her flawless skin, my face buried deep in her silken-hair.

My fantasies took me back, back to our first days, and that very first kiss.

It was almost exactly a year after I'd encountered her on the bus. The end of a twelve-month ritual of sympathetic magic and carefully orchestrated chance meetings, until finally, she opened herself up to me.

It was during the height of a very long, hot and clement summer, and I'll never forget the way it felt.

We had both been out for something to eat at a small, family-run restaurant on the high-street called 'Luigi's'.

The food there was better than you would expect to find in a small Cotswold town lying so far from the beaten track.

I'd not long started an apprenticeship at 'Cranston Engineering', a local air-con and ventilation company.

Their workshops were located on a small trading estate on the outskirts of town, and they would take on just about anybody who could swing a hammer.

It was a time before I discovered avenues to making money from my marionette work, but the job at Cranston's had taught me pattern-making, milling and lathe-work, and in retrospect, it was one of the best things that ever have happened to me.

It was the third time we'd been out with each other, just nine days after I'd completed the 'see me, think of me, want me' ritual, and I'd first bound and stitched our poppets together.

The moment is seared into my memories like it was yesterday.

Mari had been incredibly amorous towards me for most of the evening, her feelings guided and heightened by the binding of the dolls.

It felt other-worldly to be on the receiving end of that kind of attention from one so wholly bewitching.

We were walking from the restaurant. The setting sun was melting into the scorched horizon, underlighting skeins of striated cloud burning red in the sky ahead of us.

We strolled the length of the picture postcard high-street, witnessing in shared, comfortable silence, the spectacle before us that marked the end of, what was for me, a perfect day.

I'd made a move to hold her hand. But instead of pulling it away as I was expecting, she threaded her slender fingers through mine and squeezed.

My stomach folded into a knot, and I lost the ability to draw a steady breath.

She towed me into a shop doorway, turned and looked into me with more longing than I'd ever thought possible to see in a pair of eyes. The magic worked strong on the young and impressionable.

At that time, the airwaves were filled with Marilyn Manson and Nine Inch Nails, and Marianna was going through a phase of dressing decidedly gothic—a look that particularly suited her light, alabaster skin.

She'd lightened her hair to a platinum-white and wore ivory base, which made her heavy black-lined eyes and cupid's bow lips pop from the ghostly sheen of her angelic features, like they were resolving through a mist.

I reciprocated her gaze. The iridescence of her turquoise flecked eyes reeling me in.

I watched those gloss-black lips part and present themselves to me, and un-reluctantly, I accepted and took them.

The taste of her breath washed through me like a drug, and she exhaled her want into me, softening me into some form of euphoric dream state.

We hung in the flavour of each other for what felt like a lifetime, changing my lust into love. A moment I would have been happy to remain in until our time on earth ran out.

Our knowledge and experiences of life are made up of such moments as these. they brand us, and that one sits at the very top—paramount—above all others.

The service ended, and the congregation woke to leave.

I exited the hazy murk of the church into the blinding summer sunshine.

I breathed deep to clear the musk of the spice-scented air from my lungs, then noticed Mari stood across the way, clear of the subdued, grieving mutterings of the throng, obviously awaiting my appearance.

She dipped her head slightly and smiled—beckoning me over. Gladly, I complied.

"Hiya," I said softly as I neared her.

She smiled a sad, regretful smile. "Hey," she whispered, stepping forwards to give me a cautious hug.

I could see Kirsty hanging in the background, watching us with concern.

I glanced across at her. "Oh, she means well," Marianna said, "she's only worried about me."

I turned back, looked into her eyes and smiled. "I know. She's a good friend."

"Yes, she is," she agreed.

I stared into her. "I've missed you," I said, softly.

I could see the same words poised on her lips, but she was visibly holding them back—perhaps not yet ready to risk complicating her life again, probably still unnerved by her discovery at the house.

But I could tell, the dance of the poppets was already beginning to work its invisible magic, despite only being a few moves in.

"Sad day," I said—she nodded. "But you're looking well. It's lovely to see you again; I just wish it was under different circumstances."

"Me too," she agreed, dropping her eyes.

"But you look nice, Mari. Really nice."

"Thank you. You too," she replied—looking me up and down. I smiled, inside and out. "Are you going to the crematorium?" she asked.

I see-sawed my head indecisively. "Erm—I'm not sure I can; I actually have a job I need to deliver."

"The Pierrot?" she asked.

"Yes, the Pierrot," I confirmed.

I was amazed to discover she actually took notice of my work. "So, I may have to drive up there today and drop it off," I explained. A lie, but it felt right to cut loose while I was ahead. Part on this moment of mutual fondness and let the magic do the rest.

We hugged again to part our ways, but this time, her embrace seemed to be given more freely and with more warmth.

I mouthed 'bye' across at Kirsty, who was still hovering in the wings. She allowed a smile to hide her obvious concerns, and I strolled back to my car.

I glanced back just the once, hungry for one last look at my Marianna's angelic features, and to my surprise, my eyes met hers. We exchanged coy smiles and laughed with childlike abashment, and she turned to leave.

I arrived back at my car, climbed inside and dropped the fondest of smiles into my lap.

The engine fired up, and I set off for home.

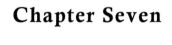

Chapter Seven

Someone Came Knocking

IF I TOOK JUST ONE THING away from the funeral, it was that now—more than ever before—I wanted her back.

I guess my arrogant complacency towards the life I'd forged had fogged my ability to appreciate Marianna for what she was, a complacency finally highlighted by her absence.

But in taking her presence in my undeserving life for granted, I'd allowed myself to lose sight of just how kind, gentle and soul-crushingly beautiful that woman actually was. A true goddess for sure. A siren. The queen of all woman, and I missed her dearly.

I needed to ramp up the intensity of the ritual of the dolls to guarantee winning her back and fast.

Instinctively, I knew that Kirsty—being the sort of friend she was—would work tirelessly to force Mari to question her strangely reigniting feelings towards me, and I couldn't allow that to happen.

I 'needed' her, I 'yearned' for her, and nothing, but nothing could be allowed to stand in the way of that.

The particular form of poppet magic I'd chosen to use could be considered among the simplest, mainly due to its ease of preparation.

But as basic as that method was, it could still be highly effective.

But ever since the funeral, it dawned on me that Kirsty could pose a far greater problem to accomplishing my goals than I first thought, so I needed to work fast to ramp up the intensity in the ritual's procedures.

I parked up back at the house, shut the engine off and sat in silence—pondering my next moves.

Distancing the effigies and the wall of salt alone wouldn't be enough to guarantee breaking the forces that bound a lifelong friendship. And as strong the link I'd formed between the dolls and the protagonists may have been, what I needed, was a way of injecting bad energies between them.

I decided on a course of action, a variation of a method I'd used just once before.

It would be a grim undertaking and draw on all of my grit and determination, but I knew it would work—'that' I felt sure of.

I rose from the car and entered the cottage. I tossed my keys onto the kitchen table and leant on the sink.

I peered down into the film of grease and oil swirling atop the stagnant dishwater, the iridescence of the slow morphing rainbow of colours aiding thought.

Then I noticed—images were beginning to form for me in the swirls, the same way a witch sees shapes relating to the future in the reflected flames of a candle, when observed through the ebony sheen of a scrying mirror.

The rainbow of colours in the oil rolled and collided beneath my searching gaze, and briefly, oh so briefly, resolved into the shape of an animal.

Then the tap dripped, causing an iridescent wave to expand across the surface and drown the image.

My plans had been affirmed by the forces that be. I would need an animal: A dog. A cat. Anything with a life that could be extinguished.

I ran through my mind a list of my friends and acquaintances, trying to recall those that owned pets.

But I soon came to the sane realisation that that particular path would be too treacherous, too risky. Far too risky to be a viable option. I needed another idea.

I powered up my laptop, opened a web page and typed in, 'Animal rescue centres' and hit 'enter'.

Three results that could be considered local flashed up on the screen. One of them, just six miles away.

I entered the number into my phone and called it.

The man that answered had that eagerness to assist normally only found in those new to a career path that they'd actually wanted to follow. But I also got the impression he'd worked there for quite some time, just by his apparent knowledge of the processes involved in adopting one of these creatures. So I deduced, he must be a true animal lover, with genuine concern for the fate of the animals that passed his way.

I doubt he would have been quite so keen to assist me, if he'd known my motivations.

He made the usual textbook enquiries. I told him I used to own a dog that had passed away, and that I'd been meaning to find a rescue animal to replace it.

He billed, cooed and sympathised, informing me that it would be just fine to turn up any time to look around, so I quickly changed into clothes that shouted, 'safe-and-dependable', and made my way there, not feeling like I had a moment to lose.

The drive to the shelter should have been a pleasant one. The late afternoon air was clear and crisp, and the electric-blue skies stretching above me were cloudless.

But it had been such a very long time since I'd sacrificed an animal, and the prospect of doing so again wasn't sitting well.

Then I began to laugh out loud at my own hypocrisy, having in all intense and purposes just murdered Jennifer Coulier.

But killing with your own hands—that's different, it lacks that detachment necessary to make it an easy thing to do.

It's the difference between shooting at something distant hovering in your cross-hairs and holding a gun to a head, and having the coldness of heart to pull the trigger and extinguish a life.

I was just fine with the cross-hairs.

I eventually turned into the shelter parking area. The animals inside seemed to wake from their self-pitying, hang-dog-sadness and began barking for attention.

It was as though they'd heard the unfamiliarity in the engine note approaching and instinctively knew that yet another joy-filled face was to walk through the doors and look upon them all with kind but pitying eyes and take one of them away from the loveless pens to their own, personal Valhalla. Escorted away by a Valkyrie-saviour to live a better life, in a place free of clawed mesh, cold, hard concrete and increasingly desperate cries to be noticed.

I presented myself at reception and could finally put a face to the voice on the phone.

I had been correct, the voice belonged to a man named 'Martin'. He'd worked there for thirteen years and seemed to possess a genuine care for the fate of the dogs that passed through their hands.

'I', on the other hand, didn't.

He led me through the corridors of second-hand companions. An unimpressive display of shop soiled, unwanted and returned merchandise.

Damaged but functional. 'Sold as seen' and in goodish working-order—at least at the last time of checking.

"So, I think you said you had a dog before?"

"Yes, 'Mickey'. He was a Patterdale Terrier." That was a dog my friend once owned and perfect for my lie.

"Awww. Lovely breed Patterdale's. Nice natures. What colour?"

"Mmm?"

"Colour? Black? Brown?" he asked.

"Oh, a kind of sandy colour. With flecks of grey—when it got older."

"Ah, nice. We actually had a black Patterdale in a few weeks back, but the pure breeds don't hang around long. The pure breeds and—what my colleague calls—the basket cases. They're the ones that get picked first—usually. The healthy looking mixed breeds that don't feel the need to look desperate get passed by."

"Well, that's actually exactly what I'm looking for."

"Good." He smiled—nearly cutting me off. "They're the best dogs here. Healthy and not mentally scarred. Mostly."

We traversed the corridors of desperate barks. I looked for a dog with youth and health on its side, preferably with an unlovable face to aid my need to kill it.

I saw a prime candidate, some bastard form of terrier. Small but bursting with life. The only problem was, it had what most would describe as a 'sweet face', but fortuitously, that was easily overshadowed by how much its incessant need to jump annoyed me.

But in all other ways, this thing seemed ideal for my purposes, and by a stroke of luck—or fate—it had been given all of the relevant shots and inoculations that would otherwise have delayed the process even further, and after taking the over-eager 'ball of joy' for a walk—to check our doubtful but faked compatibility—I decided I would take it.

The only spanner in the extensively overcomplicated works was that these places have incredibly exasperating systems of checks and double checks in place to frustrate the ease in which you can take one of these sorry animals home with you.

They insisted I make one more visit to see how the dog reacted to seeing me again. To check that there was the kind of bond between us that I was desperately trying to avoid.

I managed to convince them of a need to get it all done and dusted in a matter of days rather than weeks because of my busy schedule, and I think they must have been desperate to clear their backlog, because they agreed.

The two days that followed felt like a week, but I made good use of the time, tidying the house in readiness for a routine visit from the shelter, and more importantly—Marianna's return.

The visit happened, and all went by the book.

The routine in the 'life-box' drawer continued—moving the poppet, pouring the salt, until the effigy of the love of my life was just inches from my own, and the ever-fattening wall of sodium nearly spanned the entire drawer.

The day for the second visit with the mutt soon arrived, and if all went well, I'd be able to take it away with me.

I filled a bucket with water and placed it the middle of the garage. Then I set off and drove the tree-lined lanes to the rescue centre.

The second visit went as expected. The dog put on an impressive display of its lovable side to secure my 'apparent' affections, and I did likewise, displaying just how keen and loving 'I' could act towards the stupid beast.

But the dog's desperation to be chosen was matched only by its apparent inability to accurately judge character. So it all went through without a hiccup, and I loaded the beast into the car.

Martin gave the dog a patronising wave, but the animal seemed more interested in getting away from him and his childlike demeanour. "Bye, bye, Arthur. Take care," he mewed like some patronising adolescent.

Arthur? I thought, what a ridiculous name for a dog. But I wasn't planning to own the thing long enough to correct the outrage.

Martin offered me his hand to shake. "Well, good luck then—both of you. We'll be in touch."

My brow buckled. "In touch? Why would you be in touch?"

"Oh, you know, just a follow up, to check you're getting on okay with it."

"I'll be fine. He'll be fine," I said.

"It's just a phone call, that's all," he explained, "just to touch base." He began to look at me suspiciously.

"Oh, I see. Sorry. It's just I travel a lot—you know how it is. But if you call my mobile number, that'd be best."

He seemed happy enough with that, and his concern looked to melt away.

I signed the forms and thanked him, and we left.

At last, I had the final piece of the jigsaw I needed to bring Mari home to me. I figured just two more days of sympathetic contrivance would be adequate to accomplish my goal.

On the drive home, I thought of nothing else but Marianna. The curve of her spine. The feel of her skin. The life in her eyes.

The emptiness that filled the house had started getting to me. My lone presence echoed through the rooms like a wandering ghost without her there, and I had no vessel to fill with my adoration.

I arrived back at the house with the dog. It had leapt around the car like a gas molecule in a vacuum the entire journey there.

But that ability to annoy me was a gift, a gift to making my unpleasant task a far easier one to stomach.

I wasted no time; I couldn't risk a neighbour seeing the animal with me, giving me need to explain away its sudden absence.

I opened the passenger door and used my legs to block its eagerness to jump from the car and investigate its new surroundings.

I struggled to clip the lead onto its collar. "Just fucking wait will you," I snapped—impatiently.

The mutt seemed to sense my agitation and calmed just long enough to allow me to clip onto the ring on its collar. Although that agitation was a good thing, it gave me a strong foothold for the job that lay ahead.

I looked around to check I was alone and stepped back to let the thing out. But it just nosed past me at the first sight of an opening and leapt from the car.

The lead snapped tight, its own inertia lifting it from the ground. It tugged left, then right, bouncing on its back legs like a fucking pogo stick, paws pawing at the air.

But the stupid thing didn't even know where it was supposed to go, but it just kept on, throwing itself wildly against a collar tethered to a hand that was rapidly losing patience and self-control.

I slammed the door and led its pogoing frame into the garage.

At first, it looked confused, darting quizzical looks up at me as it padded about by the side of my legs, like a kid overdosed on tartrazine.

I dropped the lead, and it broke from my side and made for the bucket sat awkwardly centre of the room.

It sniffed around the perimeter of the pail, nudged the handle, then hopped its feet up on the rim and with a sniff—began lapping at the water inside.

I stood looking on and smirked at the irony.

Then I realised—the Lords. The 'Gods', they were assisting me.

I shut my eyes briefly and imagined Marianna coming through the door of the cottage, holding her bag, looking to me for forgiveness through the Arabic recurve of those sultry blue eyes.

I imagined her soft, red lips pressed against mine, the taste of her tongue in my mouth, the touch of her hands, the feel of her skin beneath the fascination of my worshiping fingers.

I opened my eyes again, steeled myself and strode to the bucket. I grabbed the back of its neck and pushed.

The shock of the unexpected pressure made it turn instinctively and try to bite my hand.

I thrust its throat down against the rim of the bucket, and it began to kick and yelp. I turned a nervous look up at the small window of the garage door. I couldn't risk one of my nosy bastard neighbours hearing the cries and running to investigate, so I pinched hard, grabbed one of its kicking back legs with my other hand and thrust its head down to the bottom of the bucket.

A tide of displaced water flooded over the rim and splashed onto the concrete, soaking my trousers.

The plastic tub erupted with the sounds of frantic scratching. Yelp-filled bubbles rising and bursting on the surface as it writhed in my hands.

A slick of yellow expanded away from the petrified animal, warming the turbulence, charging the fluid with the negativity of its fear and confusion. Infusing the liquid death with the bad energies seeping from its panicked body as it met an unfair end to the tune of my determined grip.

Its lungs finally flooded, and the bubbles ceased.

It fought for a short time longer, then stopped.

The tension left its neck and dissipated into the water, and I let go.

Its limp body curled and sank into the bucket. I was exhausted and felt glad it was over.

But I had what I'd set out to make. 'Unholy-Water' is what I called it. A liquid—clear only in appearance—but stained with the very essence of violent death. Charged like battery acid with fear, dread, confusion and helplessness.

I struggled to my feet and reached up to grab a roll of bin bags off the shelf.

I unrolled one and snapped it free.

My wet trousers clung to my legs as I lifted the dead dog from the bucket, water cascading off its face as I dropped it into the bag.

I knotted the end and dumped it to one side and put the roll of bags back on the shelf.

A row of clean jam jars sat neatly on the side, kept there for purposes such as this. I took one in hand and removed the lid.

I submerged the glass into the water. The fluid sucked over the rim and with a gurgle, filled.

I replaced the lid and lifted it into the light to inspect it.

I filled a few more of the jars and marked them, 'U-W' and put them back on the shelf, before tipping the rest of the water away and stowing the bucket.

I closed the garage, locked the car and carried one of the jars up to the house.

I made some tea to settle my nerves and sat at the kitchen table, peering through the steam rising from the mug at my new acquisition. "Tomorrow," I said out loud, "she'll be back tomorrow."

It grew dark, and the kitchen gradually fell into pitch blackness, but I hadn't noticed, too lost in my dreams.

I'd thought of nothing else but Marianna, a rolodex of my fondest memories of our best times: the first time she'd held my hand. The first time we'd kissed. The first time she pushed the pert, firmness of her body against mine. And the first time she let me take her.

I finally broke from my memories and noticed the darkness engulfing me.

I turned to check the time on the cooker clock, it read 8:18 PM, and I had a move to make.

I took up the jar of water and made for the cellar, slapping the kitchen lights on as I hurried past the switch.

I dropped into the cold comfort of the workshop, flicked on the lamp and pulled out the drawer beneath the cabinet.

I knelt and once again focussed my thoughts on Mari's return, visualising me and her together, back the way things were, I could almost smell her. I moved her poppet.

I carefully extended the wall of salt until it bridged the entire drawer, then unscrewing the lid of the jar, began splashing the water into the now sizeable void between the effigies of the lifelong friends. The salt granules soaked up the liquid like a sponge and began to crystallise.

Just two more moves and it would be done. It was all drawing so near I could taste it.

I quickly splashed some more of the liquid-negativity around the poppet of Kirsty for good measure, then slid the drawer back under.

I lay on my side in an empty bed, clutching Mari's pillow and a pair of her knee-length boots.

The comforting familiarity of the scent of her hair, together with the woodiness of the leather, worked to lower my body's rhythms, and I began to drift off to sleep.

My phone rang out and woke me—I'd received a message.

My hand fumbled towards the sound and grabbed the phone off the side-table. I thumbed it on.

The screen flashed on, blinding me. I lay squinting until my eyes adjusted to the light.

I scrolled through to the messages—it was from Marianna?

I sat up in bed, turned on the bedside lamp and opened the message.

Hi, Sammy. I'm sorry for messaging so late; I'm hoping you have your phone on silent if you're already in bed, the way you normally do.

Anyway, I just wanted to say hi and tell you I've been missing you, and it would be nice if we could talk some time.

Me and Kirsty fell out tonight, over something and nothing, but I'm sure it'll be fine in the morning.

I hope you're doing okay; I'm thinking of you.

Sleep well.

M X

My heartbeat pounded in my neck, and I smiled so wide it hurt my cheeks.

I considered the feelings of joy rising through me were well worth the life of the dog and helped to kill the guilt I was feeling for my actions.

I resisted replying, but I would do so in the morning, after she'd spent the night with me on her mind.

I switched off the light again, lay down and pulled the pillow and the boots in close.

My eyes closed above smiles, and I slept the sleep of the departed.

The next morning arrived and the air felt different—positively charged and strangely optimistic.

I rose from the bed, slipped on my jeans, threaded myself into my favourite t-shirt and made my way downstairs.

I turned on the oven and peered through the window to check the weather. A blanket of cloud obscured the sun, but it looked thin.

I made my way down to the draw to make the penultimate move.

I shifted the doll, poured the salt and splashed a great jarful of the unholy-water into the widening, no-man's-land void dividing the effigies.

Her doll was so close to mine now they were all but touching. Just one more inch, and they'd be together.

I had a needle and thread and a length of ribbon soaking in a bowl of rosewater, in readiness for the final move, and I couldn't wait to make it.

I climbed to the kitchen again, laid some sausages out on a baking sheet and slid them into the oven.

My phone lay on the table, impossible to ignore. I sat, took it up and opened Marianna's last message to read it one more time.

I pressed 'reply', and typed my response.

Hey, Mari. It's so nice to hear from you.

I'm so sorry to hear you and Kirsty fell out, but I'm sure it'll be fine, whatever it was.

I'm really missing you too. I'm sorry that my mum's stupid old wives' tale/doll thing upset you. It's just a daft game we used to play together when I was a kid. She was into that sort of thing, and I guess it rubbed off on me, it really didn't mean anything…

Anyway, I miss you being around. But I'll always be here if you need anything, okay.

Take care of yourself.

Sam X

I sent it, and placed the phone gently back down on the table. I was particularly pleased with the Mum/doll bullshit, it somehow belittled her reaction to discovering it, without the need to resort to ridicule.

I needed to fill my day, to stop the apprehension from eating me alive. I'd gone through a similar experience two decades earlier, the very first time I'd forced her affections.

I also needed to send the finished Pierrot to the client, having told Marianna I'd had to deliver it. It wouldn't exactly be a trust-builder if she returned home, only to find it still there. So that's how I would fill what was destined to be an anxious day.

I carefully boxed the finished puppet and drove into town. I dropped it off at the post office on the high-street.

The town seemed busy, and the sun's radiance finally burned the morning clouds away, and the atmosphere turned decidedly summery.

The clement weather began coaxing the day-trippers out to walk the streets of the chocolate box town centre, giving the place a distinctly holiday feel. It was times like these that I loved my life in Bradlington.

The uncrowded skies made it easy to smile, and I took a walk in the park to clear my head. But the hours dragged, and all I could think about was that final move.

I filled the afternoon with teashops and walks by the river to distract my mind. I daren't go home for fear of rushing the final stage and potentially ruining nearly two weeks of patient work.

I thought of a new puppet I wanted to make and bought a pad and pencil from the newsagents to start designing it.

I dined at The White Lion—three courses—which took me to 6:22, and that was it. Enough. I could wait no longer.

I drove home sedately to prolong the time. It just felt good to be traveling back, and that made it easy to eek it out.

I parked up, locked the car and entered the house. The lure of the drawer pulled me down the staircase into the cellar.

Carefully, I drew out the box for the final time and looked down into the miniature world I controlled.

I took in a deep, lungful of air and breathed it out again. I drowned my mind with thoughts of Marianna—entering the house, walking to me, taking hold of me, pressing herself against me, fucking me.

I emptied the entire bag of salt crystals into the void between the dolls, then poured the unholy-water along it and around the poppet of Kirsty.

"Come home to me, Marianna, come home. You see only me; you want only me. Come to me," I chanted, over and over again.

I slid the doll of Marianna the final inch until it was touching mine, then lifted the ribbon and the cotton—dripping with rosewater—from the bowl and carefully bound the poppets.

I stitched their hands and faces together for good measure and lay them—'us'—back in the drawer.

It was done.

I made a fire in the living room to chase back the chill of the evening. The wood crackled and fizzed, sending twists of orange flame up the chimney stack.

Images of a couple caressing, began to form in the hot, flickering vortex.

I watched the flames dance together before my fascinated gaze, sharing in each other's warmth and tenderness.

I sat in the dark in my high-backed chair, just watching the flames make love. Just waiting. And watching.

I suddenly woke. I looked at the clock on the mantle—10:47.

There was a knock at the back door; I leant forwards and turned a look towards the sound.

The knock came again. Soft. Hesitant.

I rose from the seat and made my way through the kitchen to the back door and opened it.

The unmistakable silhouette of Marianna was stood in the shadows of the doorway before me, backlit by a low-hanging moon, hidden beneath the umbrella of darkness its white light created.

We said nothing, just looked at each other.

My gut squirmed like a trapped animal, and I greeted her with a tentative smile.

I moved back from the door to invite her in. She stepped from the shadow into the light, and I took her bags from her.

The look in her eyes said it all—she was home, 'mine' again, and this time, I was determined I wouldn't mess things up.

She stared at me with lost eyes, her cheeks streaked with tears and rivers of makeup.

I wrapped myself around her unhappiness and held her. She smelled so good.

She peered up at me within the embrace. Her lips gravitated to mine, and we kissed. For the first time in weeks, we kissed.

No words were said. No words were needed to be said. We each held what we each desired, and we desired what we held.

Chapter Eight

The Return of the Goddess of Love

NOTHING ELSE EXISTED that night but me and my Marianna.

Few words were, or needed to be spoken. We held entire conversations with searching looks, understanding smiles, and soft, caressing touches.

We spoke only of a broken friendship and of my happiness at seeing her again, but outside of that, all there was to break the silence of the house was the crackling of the fire and the thumping of my happy heart.

The detached look in her eyes had returned, and I had to remind myself— she was there only because of what was hidden away in that drawer.

Her looks were through me, not really at me. Her smiles—distant and detached.

But none of that mattered to me, my grateful arms cocooned a beauty not many get chance to caress, and I never wanted to let her go, ever again.

The bed no longer felt empty, and we resisted cheapening the moment with anything as crass or vulgar as sex; we just held each other close, and I listened to her breathing as we drifted away into sleep.

I awoke the next morning, arm draped over her tiny waist, my foetal body folded around hers. Locked together like pieces of a puzzle.

I buried my nose in her neck. My eyes rolled at the euphoric scent.

She woke and twisted her head around to look back at me.

I froze, waiting to see if the look in her eyes had changed But she gazed through me with the same thousand-yard longing she had the night before, and I smiled my relief and pulled her in tight.

It was a Saturday, and by luck, or by fate, Mari wasn't working that particular day.

That morning, we sealed our love. We gave ourselves to each other, and we each took what we wanted.

I rose and showered, then left her in the bed to go and make breakfast—her wet lips and glistening skin still strong in my mind.

I cooked to the sound of her showering above me, images of her soap-drenched body crowding my elated thoughts.

We sat and ate, our silence strangely comfortable, like nothing had ever happened. But oddly, I felt bad about her broken friendship.

I'd liked Kirsty on the day we talked, and I also knew an awkwardness between them would affect our social lives. And besides, I wanted my Mari to be happy.

So, I hatched a plan. I would contrive to be seen to be the orchestrator of their rekindled friendship, to bring them back together and heal the wounds of their falling out.

I felt sure that would put me in a new, better kind of light in the eyes of Kirsty, and then by association, the rest of Marianna's circle of friends.

That weekend passed as one of the most idyllic I can remember there ever being. Idyllic enough to make me want to change—be a better person—have her with me 'not' just because of the spells I'd cast, but because she'd grown to truly respect and love me. Love me for who I am, not what I'd done.

On the Sunday, we drove to 'The Rollrights', a neolithic stone circle on the outskirts of a small, Cotswold town called Chipping Norton. A much favoured site of the Druids and Pagans in the area.

The views across the hills on the approach to the site were long reaching and blissful, but they might as well have been the crumbling buildings of a rundown city for all the attention I gave them. It was all I could do to not just stare across at Marianna.

The site was everything I'd hoped it would be; there was a calming energy in the stones you could feel when you touched them, bridging the gaps between each one like interlinking arms. The stones were many but existed as one.

I secretly gathered some soil from within the circle while Mari was distracted by the views—something new for my drawer of 'stuff', and unbeknownst to her, the primary reason we were there in the first place.

I bagged the new asset in my rucksack and joined Marianna's side to soak up the views, then we drove into the town centre to look around and find somewhere nice to eat.

We found a place we both liked the look of, a quaint bistro restaurant on a corner in the centre of the main shopping area. We were shown to a table and handed menus.

The place had a mix of modern and olde-worlde charm you often find in Cotswold towns. Small enough to be intimate but large enough to have a light, airy atmosphere.

We chose our food and placed our orders, then it was time to sow the seeds of my latest project.

I looked across the table at Marianna, purposefully pinching quizzical eyes as an opener to the conversation.

Marianna noticed and looked somewhat intrigued by the look hanging in my gaze. Her eyes inviting me to present my thoughts. "There's something I've been meaning to talk to you about," I said.

She responded with a look of concerned curiosity. "Okay?" she replied, dipping her voice.

"Your falling out with Kirsty, was it because of me?"

She hung uneasily in my question. "No, it's. No," she said—stumbling over the awkwardness.

"Listen, I don't mind if it was," I explained. "If she *did* say anything about me, it's because she was looking out for you. And maybe she doesn't know me as well as you do."

She cocked her head and reached out a hand to grab mine. "Oh, Sammy, it's really not like that."

Her brows twisted in that fondly pitying way. "You can be so lovely and so understanding sometimes." She sighed—the buttery affection in her voice sounding genuine to my ears.

I crimped a smile her way. "You two have been friends for as long as I can remember, and that shouldn't end because of some stupid misunderstanding."

"I know," she muttered. "I just didn't like the way she was badmouthing you and sticking her unwanted oar in."

I knew it, that bitch 'was' trying to interfere. But no, I was trying to change, I had to try to be more understanding—be 'the new me'. "I know, and she shouldn't have done that," I said, "but don't be too hard on her. Give it time okay. Just know that she probably meant well—I'm sure of it."

She squeezed my hand and tilted an appreciative smile across the table at me. "Thank you," she mouthed, barely audible, even to my thirsty hearing.

The food arrived.

We had sex in the restrooms to end our meal, her blood-red-painted fingernails gripping the cistern, cascades of hair tumbling down her back, as we rolled and pulsed in the moment.

We exited the stalls looking undone. The tips of our hair—stained dark by our shared perspiration—clung to reddened faces, and anyone seeing us would have known the covert moment we'd just shared.

It was all like new love again, exciting and fresh. Heartfelt and entirely relevant.

We made our way home.

The weekend had passed like a dream through a slumbering mind and drew to the most perfect of ends by discovering news of a thirteen-puppet contract from a European client waiting for me on the answering machine on our return. We celebrated.

The next day, Marianna left for work. She was a sort of a greeter/receptionist at one of these trendy hair salons in town. She was organised and had an airy gift of chat that suited such a position.

I had to drive into town myself to purchase materials for the new, upcoming job, and I decided while I was there, I'd drop by Kirsty's shop and play the part of 'the caring friend she greatly misunderstood'.

I parked on the high-street and made my way there.

I peered through the window, apart from Kirsty, the shop looked empty. Not unusual for a Monday morning—I guess.

I entered, and bell above the door rang out my presence.

Kirsty's attention lifted from the newspaper she was leant over, and she started—visibly—at the sight of me entering.

I smiled wide to waylay her unease and confusion at my arrival. "Hi, Kirsty," I called—softly—with happiness in my eyes, "I was just passing. Have you got a minute?"

Her brows flickered; she looked confused, but also intrigued. "Yeah? Yes, of course," she replied, closing the paper and sliding it to one side.

I meandered through the shelves of pointless tat and approached the counter.

I hovered in front of her, pretending to compile my thoughts, to give the impression I cared how what I was about to say would sound. But I'd rehearsed my script the whole way there and had it down pat.

I huffed a thoughtful sigh. "Listen, I know you and Mari have fallen out, and I also know why," I revealed, giving her a knowing look.

Her cheeks flushed pink, a look of 'get me out of here' galvanising her expression.

"It's okay," I assured her with a calming blink of my eyes. "Look. I know I'm probably not good enough for Marianna, and I probably don't deserve to be with someone as wonderful as *she* is. But for whatever reason, she loves me, and maybe, just *maybe*, if you gave yourself a chance—gave *me* a chance—you might find that I'm not the person you seem to think I am."

She rolled her head. "Look, Sam. I—"

"No, please, let me finish," I said, gently cutting her off. "What I wanted to say, is this—I don't really care about any of that, well, maybe I do a bit, because, in fact, I really like you. But the reality is, I'm just one part of her life. But you two, you two have been best of friends for years, and it's wrong for you to fallout over something as insignificant as *I* am."

Her brow softened to my self-deprecation. I continued. "So I've talked to her, explained to her that you only meant well, and were, in all likelihood, only thinking of *her* happiness and *her* wellbeing." I faked pleading eyes. "So, if I got her to call you, would you please answer and try and make up? For me?" I looked her in the eyes. "I'm really not here to get in the way of what you two have and have *always* had."

She melted before me like ice cream in the sun; I could see tears of compassion licking at her eyes. "Oh, Sam, I'm sorry. I'm so, so sorry. You're right. Maybe—in reality—I don't think *anyone* is good enough for her. And maybe I do have a tendency to stick my nose in and where it isn't wanted."

I smiled knowingly and laughed lightly. "Well, maybe. Just a little."

She seemed to free herself of her embarrassment and joined in the mirth. But part of me wanted to throttle her.

But no, this was the 'new' me, the 'new' start, a 'new' beginning.

She walked from behind the counter and approached me, wrapping her arms around my shoulders. She felt good in my reciprocated embrace, and her scent was sweet.

"I'll talk to her, okay," I whispered.

We parted, and I backed away from the counter to a fanfare of grateful smiles. "Thank you, Sam," she called, as I reached the door.

I looked back and smiled coyly. "You're welcome," I said, and with a tinkle of the bell—left.

My performance was perfect, wholly convincing in its levels of sincerity, I felt sure of that.

But then I thought—*was I actually acting?* Half of what I'd said, and felt, seemed to come out naturally. Not the usual verbatim facsimile of actions I'd observed in others and presented as my own, as I normally would. But real, more from the heart.

Had I just witnessed what it is to be truly compassionate? Was I 'becoming' more human?

I 'was' aware of a difference, even if I couldn't quite work out exactly what it was.

I made my way through the high-street to the salon. *Why wait to show Marianna how nice and understanding I can be*—I thought, feeling a kind of pride for my newfound ability to react, rather than act.

I swung the door open and stepped tentatively inside the caustic, shampoo atmosphere of the salon. It clung the backs of my teeth and scolded my nose like a line of coke.

I knew it wasn't considered the done thing in the everyday world to pay visits to your partner during workhours, but it 'was' the first time I'd ever done so, and the surprise in Marianna's face as she noticed me entering displayed that.

Just two women sat in chairs being tended to. One with foil squares folded into her hair, the other sat addressing her stylist in the mirror, spewing some brand of gossip about a problem neighbour, while the disinterested girl crawled all over her, snipping locks from her animated head.

But both women shared a slight unease at my presence, maybe it's because I obviously wasn't gay, and as women, they looked undone in their plasmic states of preen?

Marianna rounded the counter wearing a quizzical smile. "What are you doing here?" she asked as she stretched up to peck me on the cheek.

"Oh, nothing much really. I won't keep you long, I can see you're busy," I assured her.

I quietly closed the door and walked her to one side. "I've just been up to see Kirsty," I said.

Her face dropped like a rock. "You did *what*!"

"No. Listen. It's all right," I said. "We talked, and I actually think she kind of warmed to me. Anyway, I told her that you two have been friends forever, and that I didn't want her view of me to get in the way of that. So, would you *please* call her? She's expecting you to."

Her face displayed her mild abhorrence and confusion at what I'd done. But I could also see her softening to the idea. "Okay. I'll call her," she muttered—thoughtfully.

Then I remembered—the dolls! The fucking dolls! I needed to adjust the dolls.

In my haste to be the hero, I'd forgotten about their set-up in the life-box.

I needed to remove the barrier that had split them in the first place and bring them together again, or any attempt at reconciliation would prove fruitless.

"Erm? Well, maybe leave it an hour," I said, "she looked like she was in the middle of something, so maybe leave it until lunchtime."

She listened to me, then hung in her thoughts for a moment. "Yes, okay. Good idea," she agreed.

I turned to walk to the door, but I was halted by a tug on my shirt. Marianna pulled me back behind a dividing screen, her eyes burning with mischief.

She cupped my face in her hands and looked me square in the eyes. "Thank you," she said—the sincerity in her voice palpable—then deliberately, placed the gentlest of kisses on my mouth, before leaning back and carefully wiping the sticky gloss coating from my lips with her tiny, delicate thumb.

I winked and left through the door.

My legs thundered beneath my panic as I sprinted to the car.

I rushed for home—driving like a veritable Schumacher. I had to clear away the salt barricade in the drawer, and quick, or their attempts to reconcile would be met with failure, and *my* attempts to wear the glory of my kindness and understanding would fall flat on its face.

I arrived back at the house and ran from the car, leaving the engine running, keys hanging in the ignition.

I burst through the door, thundered down the steps into the cellar, pulled out the draw and began frantically scooping the thick, crusty wall of salt from between the poppets.

I didn't have days or even minutes to properly undo my ritual, so I just doused the poppet of Kirsty with what remained of the rosewater in the bowl on the shelf and slid it across the box until it was touching the poppet of Marianna.

I took up the needle and the thread and began frantically whip-stitching the poppets together.

All I could do was hope, that with my and their own good will on side, it would be enough.

I ran to my shelves and took up another jar, of rose, cinnamon and Shatavari-infused water down from the shelf, and for good measure, began sprinkling it over all three of the dolls lying huddled together in the life-box.

I released a pent sigh of relief and slid it back under the cabinet.

I had done what I could, time would out my success, or my failure.

Chapter Nine

A New Romance

THE TWO WEEKS THAT FOLLOWED couldn't be described as anything other than wonderful, and I spent it wearing a look of utter contentment across my face.

The reconciliation of a lifelong friendship was a success, and I was to be seen in a far better light as a result.

Not long after Marianna's return to my arms, the weather had taken a brief turn for the worse, a short spell of cold, wintery temperatures and thunderous rainstorms that passed as quickly as they came, giving way to hot, late-summer days.

But the potentially searing heats were tempered by a cool, autumnal breeze, and the short, inclement spell had washed the wasps and their incessant, bothersome natures from the skies, giving the burgeoning autumn air all of the optimism of spring, prompting many to dig out the barbecues once more, filling the streets with the charred scents of marinaded flesh.

One late-afternoon—Kirsty messaged me. She was holding a sort of garden party/gathering at her place and was inviting—or more accurately—'insisting' that me and Mari attend.

I confess, it warmed me to the core to discover—upon raising the subject that evening—that Marianna knew nothing of the planned get-together, until I'd told her.

Was messaging me, a display of new trust? A gesture made to brush aside hard feelings? If it was, it worked.

I typed our acceptance to the invite with a strange form of elation swimming within me. 'I' had been invited to a party by 'Kirsty Green'—one of the cool and attractive girls from school.

It was a brand-new feeling for me, and I wasn't exactly sure how to handle it.

Sure, I'd been to gatherings with that crowd before but only due to my association with Marianna, and I supposed, in reality, this was too.

But no, this 'was' different, she'd asked 'me', and to my mind, that marked a new form of acceptance into their group.

The gathering itself wasn't until just over a week later, and I was way ahead of the game on the marionette job, the joy at having my Marianna back somehow making my work-rate soar. So, I suggested we go away for a long weekend.

The resulting shockwaves that had rippled through our lives by Mari discovering my drawer had blown away any chance we had to book a holiday that year. So I thought—four days away together might in some way make up for that. So that's what we did.

I booked us a room in a hotel overlooking the ocean in the small Cornish resort of St Ives.

Marianna always had a keen interest in art, and I knew the town itself housed at least three galleries of some notoriety, including a satellite branch of the 'Tate'.

Tregenna Castle was also only a short drive away, and that alone was enough to spike my interest in the place. So we packed the car and set off.

The drive there took nearly six hours, but none of those hours seemed even to registered in my conscience. I just drove, my left hand resting on Mari's leg, a comforting reminder that she was back with me.

We dropped down on the M5 motorway, then picked up the A30.

The road was long and straight, at least compared to the majority of roads in Britain. We could almost have imagined we were on some Route 66 style, endless American highway.

The air was warm, and I lowered the roof on the Merc.

Mari rode the late-summer breeze like a roller-coaster, her arms in the air, golden tresses rolling in the billowing wind as we traversed the open roads.

The day turned to night, and the sky above us dimmed to a deep-blue vista of stars and constellations, untroubled by an absence of manmade lighting to dilute their crisp beauty.

Eventually, we arrived.

The hotel itself existed in a mix of classic seaside quaintness and modern, contemporary chic.

Our room was large and high ceilinged in that way old Georgian buildings were, the long windows lording over an Atlantic Ocean you only knew was there by the sound of its crashing waves fizzing on the sands, and the flashes of starlight glinting off the peaks of the relentless swells rolling shorewards.

We unpacked and flopped on the bed together, exhausted by the drive but happy to finally be there—together.

I made us some tea, we drank it, then wrapped ourselves around each other and drifted off to sleep.

Over the following four, perfect days—we walked the sands of Porthmeor Beach. Surmised the hidden meanings peppering the diverse work in the Sculpture Gardens. Traversed the endless corridors of brilliant, yet divisive works of art lining the dozens of art gallery walls and absorbed the sun's ethereal brilliance.

We ate in the best restaurants, drank the finest wines and took in views that had inspired generations of visiting artists for centuries before us.

But as beautiful, breath-taking and awe-inspiring as all of those things were, they were all eclipsed by the glowing presence and un-tethered beauty of Marianna. The love of my life.

On the final day, we took a last, long walk along the town's sea-front to take a few last photos. But it was impossible to resist turning the lens Marianna's way, and she ended up gracing every single picture.

The journey home seemed to pass much quicker than the one there. Mari slept most of the way, and as nice a time as we'd had, it was still comforting to arrive back to the familiarity of our lovely, idyllic, little sandstone cottage.

The day of the garden party finally arrived. It was a Sunday, and despite the Saturday being extremely wet, it had cleared up and dried by the time we were getting ready to leave the house.

We crossed through the town and turned into Cope Street and were faced by a sea of cars lining the entire road.

Kirsty always had been an incredibly popular girl, and it seemed that popularity meant the neighbours would have to park a short walk away for the next few hours. But by a stroke of luck, someone was just leaving, and we quickly grabbed the space.

I rounded the car and opened the door for Marianna. She swung her slender legs out and rose majestically into the day.

She had a short, white summer dress on and cute little trainers. She looked adorable.

Barbecue smoke lifted skywards from behind Kirsty's house, and we could hear the murmur of voices drifting up the street, along with the smell of burning sausage meat.

We made our way to the side gate brandishing a bottle of Pino, let ourselves in and were intercepted by a semi-inebriated Kirsty who looked genuinely happy to see us arrive.

"You made it," she cried, as she trotted over and threw her arms around the both of us.

She was accompanied by her dog, a smallish west-highland terrier, who bounced around her legs like it was on elastic.

I crouched down to greet it. It bounded over to me and instantly turned sedate. It began sniffing my left hand, the hand that had held the dog beneath the water.

It stepped back and turned distrusting eyes up at me. Could this dog smell the fear and murder staining my fingers?

"Ohhh, look how calm he is around you. He must really like you," cooed Kirsty. "He usually just jumps around. That's amazing."

But the dog looked anything but trusting, it stared into me, it knew, knew what I'd done and knew what I was.

Maybe Kirsty was too drunk to see it, but I was eager to break free the dog's accusatory stare before anyone noticed.

We ambled into the garden; it was much larger than the outside of the house would've suggested. I'd been once before, but it seemed much bigger than my memories.

Pockets of gossip and laughter mottled the lawn, and a clandestine huddle of males surrounded the glowing charcoals, occasionally ducking beneath a drifting blanket of smoke to turn an eclectic mix of singed meat products.

Kirsty began to point and list the names of all the people there, names I'd never normally absorb into my disinterested mind. But that day, I wanted to try to change all of that. Show an interest, be a friend, not just the passing acquaintance I usually presented myself as.

I recognised many of the people from the funeral. I nodded their way whenever we made eye contact, and they respectfully reciprocated with a smile and a raise of their glasses and beer bottles.

I had to admit—after everything that had happened—it was simply nice to be there, to feel part of something, instead of on the fringes, as I'd always been before.

I pondered what the difference even was. And concluded it was simply feeling welcome.

We continued our tour of recognition. "There's Sally and her partner James. Oh, and over there, that's Natalie and—is that Emma? Yes, Emma. Hi, girls!" she shouted.

They lifted waves above their beaming faces and returned the greeting. "Oh yeah, and *Mark's* here," she sang, in a tone that purported that what she'd said was somehow unusual. "Mark! It's Marianna," she called.

A face I didn't know turned to face us and brightened at the sight of Mari. "Helllloooo," he cried, acting strangely surprised to see her there. Or was it happiness?

He put down his plate on the table he was stood by and made his way across the lawn to greet us, wiping his hands on the back of his trousers. "Maz," he chirped.

I'd never heard anyone else call her 'Maz' before. "It's nice to see you outside of work for once," he said as he neared us, or more accurately, 'her'. "I didn't know you were coming, I thought you were away?"

"Oh. I was. *We* were. But only for four days. We came back on Friday," she explained.

I stood like a lemon on the side-lines. "Oh. Mark. This is Samuel. Sam I mean. My partner. I'm not sure you two have ever met?"

"No, we haven't," he said—extending an elegant but burly hand. "Hi, Sam, nice to finally meet you." We shook hands, but I was still none the wiser.

Marianna seemed to sense this and turned to me. "Mark is my boss, at the salon," she explained.

"Ahhhh," I exclaimed, with a toss of my head, "of course." I did recognise the name but failed to make the connection.

"Well, I'm only boss at work," he said, winking her way, "She's a great asset to me; everyone loves her," he enthused.

He was clean-cut, muscular, and I guess some would say handsome, in that slightly over-preened way that became fashionable in the nineties.

But his air and manner were light and mildly condescending. A boutique pretty-boy.

"I understand you make puppets," he proclaimed.

"Marionettes. Yes, for my sins," I replied, a pathetically standard response that embarrassed me.

"So how did you get into that?" he asked.

I wasn't sure if he was genuinely interested or just being charmingly polite? But I proceeded to either interest, or bored him to tears with a fairly extensive answer to see if I could make him yawn.

But he didn't, he 'did' actually seem quite fascinated in what I had to say. One of life's very real charmers.

A glass rang out like a pre-emptor to a wedding speech. Everyone turned their bemusement towards the sound and saw Kirsty standing on a crate by the shed.

"Can I just have everyone's attention for a second," she asked, in a softly apologetic voice.

Everyone put their conversations on hold and turned their interest to face her.

"I just wanted to thank you all for coming and say how lovely it is to see you all here." Her facade turned morose. "I also wanted to quickly ask you all to raise a toast to someone who, for obvious reasons, couldn't be here today, and I for one dearly miss her company. Could we all please raise our glasses to our absent friend, Jennifer, who I'm sure we all greatly miss."

Everyone grabbed their drinks from their resting places, lifted them respectfully skyward and collectively murmured, "To Jennifer."

The air went quiet while everyone took a sip from their drinks. But all I could focus on was Kirsty's dog just sat core of the sombre silence, staring at me from the farthest side of the garden, fixing me with a knowing stare.

That little fucker knew, I don't know how, but it knew.

The party rolled along at a walking pace. We promenaded the garden, relaying the same, mundane conversations, to a mixed variety of mundane people. But for all of that, it 'was' just nice to be there.

I kept pondering the question, 'are dogs psychic?'. But then I realised, the one from the shelter sure as hell can't have been.

Or maybe it was. Maybe it was simply blinded by its desperation to be chosen and taken away from that place and that Christianesque do-gooder Martin?

But whatever the situation with that particular mutt, the dog that spent the entire afternoon just watching me from the far-side of the lawn certainly was; he could read me like a novel and didn't seem to warm to the stories hidden within my pages.

Marianna excused herself from my side to go and chat to an old friend. I perched on a table and just watched the mechanics of the gathering reciprocate before me.

Kirsty's eye caught mine, and she smiled with the warmth of a summer breeze, then made her way across to end my solitude. "Hi, lonesome," she said, softly, "are you okay?"

"Yeah, I'm good, thanks." I smiled.

She parked her pert backside on the table next to me. "I just wanted to say thank you for what you did; it was really very kind of you."

"That's all right," I replied. "I just wanted you two to be happy."

"I know, and that's why I feel so awful. I guess I 'did' have you all wrong, and I apologise for that."

She barged a pally shoulder into mine, stood from the table and leant into me, kissed me on the cheek and wrapped her free arm around my shoulder. "Sorry," she whispered into my ear.

"That's okay," I whispered back.

She stepped out of the hold, smiled, rubbed my shoulder affectionally and took up her mingling duties again.

I stood and walked across to join Mari's side. She seemed to be swamping the conversation with her enthusiasm at seeing her old friend again.

I recognised the girl from our school days. Mark—her boutique-boss—was stood on the perimeter of the gathering, listening, seeming happy to just hang back and observe the reunion.

But he seemed to be looking at Marianna more than I would have considered the usual amount. Mind you, she did look fucking incredible, so why wouldn't he?

I had wondered earlier if he might be gay, what with being a hairdresser—but obviously not.

Marianna finally noticed me hovering in the wings. "Oh. Jane. This is Samuel; he also went to our school."

The girl looked through me like I was made of crystal. "Ohhh, yeahhhh, I do kind of recognise you," she bullshitted, her eyes as blank as a sheet of paper.

111

Mari smiled fondly back at me with her distant eyes and grabbed my arm. "Yeahh, he's my partner; we've been together forrrrr? Twenty years now," she said. I nodded to affirm her words.

But the girls face said it all. I nearly started laughing. Her eyes screamed 'What the fuck are you doing with *him*?' One of the most heart-stoppingly gorgeous woman anyone is ever likely to lay eyes on, stood, clutching the arm of a dweeb who makes fucking puppets for a living.

The party eventually began thinning out, then drew to an end.

We both hung back to help clear up. Fill bin bags. Put things away. Load the dishwasher.

We thanked Kirsty for a great time. She gave me a hug, a kiss and a cheeky wink, and we left.

"Did you have a nice time?" Marianna asked.

"Yeah, it was nice, wasn't it?" I replied. "She's nice Kirsty; I like her a lot."

"Yeah, she is lovely. I can't *believe* we fell out."

"I know. Never mind, it's all good now," I said.

She smiled across at me. "Thanks to you."

"You're welcome, ma'am," I replied.

We sat in one of our comfortable silences while I drove us home. Then I had a question to put forward.

"So, what's the deal with Mark then? Why wasn't his partner with him?" I asked, in a kind of forced, semi-disinterested tone.

"Mmm? Oh Mark, I'm not sure, I think he's single at the moment? He *was* seeing someone, not that long ago, but I think that went south? Or maybe it didn't? We don't really talk much about that stuff. "

I fished some more. "Oh yeah, why, what was wrong with her? Or was it him?"

She laughed. Not a titter, a full-on belly laugh—not that Mari had a belly to speak of. "Are you getting all jealous? Are you? Is my Sammy getting all jealous of my boss Mark? Hmmmmm?" She slapped my arm with the back of her hand. "He's as straight as they come. A *reeeeal* lady's man, and women *loooove* him," she enthused. "He's really quite irresistible."

She sat looking forwards with a deadpan face. "Not all hairdressers are gay, you know," she added.

I couldn't quite read if she was telling the truth or kidding about. "A lot of them are," I said, taking the bait.

"Well, yeah, they are. But Mark *definitely* isn't."

I hung in the iron clutches of her words. What the hell did she mean by that? Maybe nothing?

I forced a querying smirk and chuckled. "What does that mean? So he *is* a lady's man?" I tittered, but I was only laughing on the outside.

Mari adjusted herself in her seat to face me and pulled an inquisitive frown. "Are you *actually* getting jealous of Mark?" she mocked. "Are you? Is my Samuel getting all protective over his lovely, wonderful girlfriend? Hmmm?" she teased.

She began jabbing me in the ribs. "Is he? Is he feeling all threatened by my boss, is he?" She jabbed some more.

I winced and began laughing. "No. No, I'm not, I'm just—you know—curious, that's all."

She stopped jabbing and just stared at the side of my face. "Pleb." She laughed.

"Shut up, you," I retorted. "If I'm a pleb, you're a nob."

"*You're* the nob. Nob-head." She smirked, then flicked my ear. "Silly bitch."

"You're the bitch," I responded.

She smirked and sat smiling at my vain attempt to mask my insecurity.

The next month passed as happily as the previous one. I got all but two of the contracted marionettes carved, strung and painted.

I sent photos to the client, and he was so happy he paid me for those upfront, before he'd even received them.

Marianna seemed content with life. The distant look of adoration remained and we spent most weekends and many evenings walking in the beauty of the surrounding countryside, enjoying the last of the temperate weather before autumn fully took hold and began claiming the leaves off the trees.

Then, something happened.

Chapter Ten

The Collapse of the Walls of Jericho

IT WAS A SATURDAY, and we'd just sat down to eat lunch, before we were to leave for the afternoon and stroll the local antique shops to find a chest of drawers for the spare bedroom.

Then, mid-meal, the phone rang.

Mari jumped up to answer it. "Hellooo?" she warbled.

I listened. I could hear the voice on the other end of the line was somewhat high pitched; it was a girl.

"Oh, hi, Kirsty. How are you?" Mari chirped.

I chewed slowly, trying to hear the muted reply.

Kirsty Green had a carrying voice, I could just about make out the word 'pop', and I think 'coffee'?

"I'll just check with Sammy," Mari said, "hang on."

Marianna leant back into the doorway and covered the mouthpiece. "Kirsty was just going to pop over for a quick coffee," she explained. "She said she won't keep us long, and we can go out antique-hunting after. Would that be okay?"

"Of course," I replied. I'd grown quite fond of Kirsty. I liked her a great deal and would be happy to see her myself. "That'd be nice, invite her over."

The crunch of the driveway gravel announced her arrival, and her sunny disposition erupted through the back door. "Hiyaaaaa," she chimed, as she bumbled and flustered her way into the kitchen.

Her and Mari sat down at the table and began swapping gossip while I made the drinks: Emma had met a new man, but he had four children, and the rest of the girls reckoned he was just seeking a mother figure to replace his recently deceased wife.

Jackie had crashed her car—again—the third one she'd wrecked in just two years.

Jane and Tony were planning to re-take their wedding vows—for some bizarre reason I knew I'd never be able to fathom—and Philippa had broken her little toe on a speaker stand while she ran to answer her door.

But other than that, all was relatively normal.

I delivered the mugs to welcoming hands and sat down to join them.

Kirsty leant back out of the huddle to invite me to join in the conversation. "So, how are you two doing?" she asked, taking a cautious sip of her coffee.

Me and Mari looked at each other, assessing whether our answers where a match. And by the happy, distant gleam in her eyes, it appeared they were. The magic was still working, so I let her answer for me.

"Yeahhh, we're doing good. We've just both been busy—you know how it is. Sammy's nearly completed his latest puppet job, and they look fantastic."

Kirsty flashed interested eyes. "Oooo, could I take a look, after?" she asked. "Would you show me?"

"Of course," I said—happy to oblige. "I've got eleven of them done so far, just two more to go. I'll take you down in a bit and show you."

She smiled a genuine smile, actually seeming kind of fascinated by my work.

Kirsty suddenly jerked from the conversation. "Ooo, before I forget," she chirped—turning to root through her bag hanging on the back of the chair.

She drew out a brown envelope and lightly tossed it onto the table. "These are for you, I printed them out last night, they're from the party in the garden."

I took up the envelope and pulled out about a dozen or so photos that I had no idea she'd even taken.

They all had either Mari, me, or both of us in frame to some degree. From a distant, blurry shot of our backs, to a full-length close-up of us talking to other party-goers.

But I just stared at them, shuffling through the increasing horror of each picture.

It suddenly dawned on me—that for whatever reason—in our twenty years together, not many photos of us existed to chronicle our passage of time, and looking down into my hands, I suddenly knew why.

I looked so utterly out of place stood next to her. A lanky geek hanging with undeserved confidence next to one of nature's finest creations.

I shuffled the deck, desperately trying to find just one photo that painted me in a kinder light, but after passing the same pictures a third, and fourth time, I realised it didn't exist.

I looked akin to a nerdy fan grabbing a photo opportunity with his favourite, cock-stiffeningly gorgeous movie actress, and all I wanted to do was tear them up and burn them. Banish them from a reality I'd spent two decades denying.

Marianna extended an elegant hand out to me. "Let me see," she said in her soft, sweet voice.

I looked up at her, I could feel my face displaying the sickened feeling that was dragging my guts through the ground. "What's wrong, love?" she asked, with genuine concern. "What is it?"

She took the pictures from my reluctant hands and turned them to face her curiosity, to see what it was that so troubled me.

I actually contemplated snatching them back and ripping them up, as a last desperate attempt to stop her from seeing them.

She began flicking through each one, Kirsty cranking her neck to join in the viewing. "Ahhhh, these are nice," she said—getting lost in the memories. "Oh, look, there's Jane," she fizzed, pointing her pinkie towards one of the pictures.

I just looked on, helpless, like a veritable Damocles. *Maybe she'll be too interested in the other people to notice*, I thought—but then it happened.

She suddenly paused on one of the photos, two further on from the one of Jane, and I felt certain that it was one of me and her, where I looked like a turd on a plate of cakes.

Her face relaxed out of its joy, and she just gazed at the image. Her eyes briefly lifted from the picture and looked across at me, then dropped back down to the abomination she held in her fingertips.

Her brows crumpled, and she looked confused by what she saw.

I attempted to feel handsome inside, like that would somehow translate to my face. But it obviously didn't work, as she kept flicking bewildered looks in my direction.

I could see it in her eyes, the disparity between her perception of me in real life and how I appeared to her in the photos, were two completely different entities.

Her puckered expression displayed an internal battle that was obviously raging inside of her, as she tried to comprehend exactly what it was she was witness to.

It was as though the photos existed as windows to seeing through and beyond the spells I'd cast to force her affections. A two-way mirror to seeing the reality of her life and her perception of it.

119

I just wanted to remove my face from the field of conflict. "Another drink anyone?" I sang in a jovial voice, carrying my still steaming mug of tea to the sink and tipping it away.

I heard a finger-ring tap one of the mugs. "I'm fine, thanks, Sam," said Kirsty—the bewilderment in her voice audible, "mine's still hot. I've not quite finished it yet."

"Marianna?" I asked, with my back to her.

She didn't answer me at first, then eventually lifted from her 'Road to Damascus' moment. "Erm? No, I'm fine, thank you."

The next hour trickled past awkwardly, but my dented standing was slightly improved by the 'ooos' and 'ahhs' that came forth from Kirsty as I displayed to her the marionettes I'd finished. Giving me chance to showcase my not inconsiderable puppeteering skills.

Her face would always light up whenever I was gifted the opportunity to bring one of my dormant creations of wood and string to life for her and amaze her pretty, sunshine expression with how alive they could become.

The time finally arrived for Kirsty to leave, and while her and Mari clucked their parting gossip on the doorstep, I quickly scooped up the photos from the table and slid them back into the envelope.

I turned and looked around, then slipped it in amongst the letters in the rack of bills and reminders on the side-table, then joined Marianna's side to bid Kirsty a farewell.

We finally managed to leave for our shopping trip, and with the pictures out of sight and aided by the distraction of hunting down a suitable item of furniture, my standing gradually returned to more of an equilibrium, and the forces of my spells began, quite literally, to work their magic again.

Her suspicions finally seemed to wane, and the distant, adoring looks gradually returned.

The life-box was doing its work, and our otherwise mundane hunt for a utilitarian piece of furniture became strangely enjoyable in its lack of thrills.

It took me a good hour to drop off to sleep that night, still troubled by the earlier event.

Then I woke, but it was still pitch-black behind the curtains.

I lifted my hand and quietly tapped the button on my bed-side clock. '3:47 AM' lit up beneath my fingers.

I swung my arm behind me to comfort myself with a brief touch of Marianna's hip, but my hand fell on empty bedding.

I rolled my shoulders to look behind me, but the other side of the bed lay empty.

I lifted my ear from the pillow to listen, but I failed to hear any activity from the bathroom.

I jerked awake, swung my legs from under the duvet and wandered from the room to find where Marianna was.

I quietly descended the staircase into the kitchen.

The soft, ethereal glow of the under-unit lighting illuminated the kitchen work-tops. And lying there—by the kettle—was the envelope, all of the photos spread out over the cold, granite surface.

Then I heard a sound, a brushing of wood on wood and noticed a faint light spilling from the open door of the cellar.

Taking great pains to tread carefully, I descended the staircase into the chilled musk of the basement.

Some of the staircase flagstones were loose, but I knew where to step to travers unheard; I'd learned the pattern over time from my own, secret midnight excursions.

I heard drawers being opened and closed, and as I neared the last few steps, I discovered Marianna ransacking my workshop.

I stood watching her for a time, unaware of my presence.

I knew exactly what she was doing—she was seeking my new life-box, and at that point, I knew her reaction to the photos had spiked her suspicions again.

"What are you doing?" I asked, in a soft, unremarkable tone.

She screamed and pirouetted to face me like a guilty dancer, her arms flinching to the side of her face in full, morrow reflex.

"What are you doing?" I reiterated, the inquisition in my voice purposefully laced with a tone of mild disappointment.

She fell over her tongue, trying to blurt any kind of response. "I-I-I was looking f-f-for some t-tape," she stuttered.

"Some tape? What for?" was my reply to her attempt at bullshit me.

"I w-wanted to t-tape those pictures up on the wall upstairs," she stammered.

I looked at her, working my hardest to resist flicking a glance towards the underside of my materials cabinet. "What, at 3:50 in the morning?" I asked—slightly condescendingly.

I dropped off the step and walked across to my drawer of tapes—the one she'd just closed—and pulled it open again, handing her a roll. "There you go," I scorned.

She pinched it from my fingertips like she was taking a bone from a hungry dog and strained a bulimic smile, then edged around my disappointment and made her way up the stairs.

I straightened the drawers and pushed them all back in. *Fuck!* I thought, she was on to me—I was sure of it.

I rose from the cellar and shut the door. Marianna was taping the photos haphazardly on the kitchen wall, as if she had always meant to. Stupid bitch that she was, like I wouldn't see through 'that'. But she continued, uneasy beneath the weight of my crushing gaze, shying distrusting looks back over her shoulder towards me.

Then she stopped and hovered in the screaming silence.

I could see she was trying to build up some kind of resolve, some ardour. "Are you doing the doll thing again?" she asked.

Shit, I thought, what to do? Just deny it, that's all I 'could' do. "The doll thing?" I said—pretending I didn't know what she meant. "What do you mean, 'the doll thing'?"

She shook a doubting head and smirked dismissively. "You know very well what I mean. The *dolls*, are you doing the thing with the *dolls*?" she thrust.

I rolled my head, half despair, half forced ridicule. "Do you *honestly* think that some stupid old wives' thing with dolls can control your life? Do you?" I mocked. I could see my words cut her, which hurt me. "So, what the hell has brought *this* on?" I asked, knowing full well the answer.

I'd cornered her, I could see the words, 'because I'm unbelievably beautiful and popular, and you're not' poised on her lips, threatening to blurt from her perfectly formed mouth and ruin my life.

But she didn't, visibly pulling herself back from the confrontation—looking towards me through the corners of her pitying eyes.

I could tell, she felt mean for even thinking such things. At least that's what I read from her backfoot, apologetic countenance.

If nothing, behind all that perfection, Mari had a compassionate heart.

I had the upper hand, 'use it'—I thought. "I don't know what you want from me? Aren't I always good to you? Don't we have a nice life together?" I pleaded.

"I'm not doing any *doll* thing, that was just a stupid game from my childhood, it didn't mean anything, but you just won't let it go, will you?"

With her walls crumbling before me, the life-box magic began to do its thing again.

Her bellicose facade began to dissolve to the heat of my shaming, melting away into her embarrassment.

She broke from her suspicions, crossed the room and wrapped her arms around my despair. "I'm sorry, I don't know what's wrong with me. Please forgive me," she whispered, her mouth close to me ear, her soft voice vibrating through me—lifting me from the floor.

I'd gotten away with it, a second time, but the increasing frequency of these 'hiccups' had begun to trouble me.

She led me back to bed, climbed aboard my insecurities and ground them away to dust. Her lithe, toned body writhing rhythmically atop my gratitude, sat high in my hypnotised gaze, until nothing at all of our crossed words and awkwardness remained.

The following two weeks passed without incident. We lived our lives, and I finished the marionettes. I packed them, shipped them, got paid, and smiles were the standard form of expression in the cottage.

Then—hiccup number three reared its inevitable head.

It was a chilled morning, windows whitewashed by a heavy fog cloaking the entire house.

I was preparing breakfast, and Mari floated down the staircase dressed for work.

"Mmmm, that smells good. Are you eating with me?" she asked—as I dished out the component parts of an English breakfast onto hot plates.

"Of course," I replied, "I couldn't possibly flood the house with such a nice stink and resist joining you in demolishing it."

She laughed.

We sat and began eating. We'd gone to bed unusually early the night before, so woke at the crack of dawn.

It was nice having the extra time to blend into the day and not having to rush to get ready.

Then it came, like a punch to the face, or a kick to the gut.

Marianna briefly lifted from her eating routine. "Oh, yeah. I nearly forgot," she said, clearing her mouth, "I won't be back till late tonight, Mark says he's going to begin training me up as a stylist, starting this evening. He says he has plans? I guess he means for me? But he says I really need to learn at least the basics of styling for some reason? I'm not sure why? He won't tell me that yet, or exactly what his plan *is*."

She took another mouthful of food, chewed it and swallowed. "But I suppose I'll find out at *some* point what these plans are. Exciting, huh?" she said, with a gulp.

I looked on in shock. Was this it? Was this the beginnings of the affair I'd always dreaded? "You're going to start training as a hairdresser, tonight?" I asked.

It sounded so ridiculous coming from my mouth, but she didn't bat a lid.

"Yeah. Well, yeah—apparently. But anyway, I guess I'll be two or three hours later than normal, so don't wait for me to eat or anything. I'll grab something on the way home, or just eat when I get back."

I felt stunned inside. She was throwing me this bullshit without a flicker. "And how long will this be going on for?" I asked.

"Oh, I don't know. As long as it takes—I guess." She stabbed her fork in the last piece of bacon, scooped the soup of breakfast remnants onto it and wrapped her glossy, red lips around it.

She glimpsed her watch, then erupted into life. "Shhhhit. I'm running laaaaate," she sang, leaning across the corner of the table and depositing a still-chewing kiss on my cheek. "I haven't got time to do the dishes, love, just leave them in the sink, and I'll do them when I get back tonight, okay?"

I didn't answer, failing to put forward my usual reassurance to not worry, and that I'd do them.

My failure to respond as I normally would jerk her from her routine. "Sweetheart? Is everything all right?" she asked, looking down at me.

I don't know what she saw, but she dropped her bags again and crouched down before me. "Oh, sweetheart, is this because if the training? It won't be forever, and it'll be good for me. For *us*."

I forced a smile I didn't feel, just to get her away from me. "Okay. I understand," I muttered.

"Look. We'll talk more later; I have to go now; we're fully booked this morning." She kissed me again, this time, exaggerating her placement of her mouth on mine, I assume to try to quell my concerns.

I could taste the gloss-film coating her flawless lips, and for a moment, I forgot myself and drifted into my fantasies.

She released me from my dream state and smiled into my eyes. "Love you," she whispered, then rose and left through the door—leaving me alone to deal with an unquenchable feeling of dejection.

I didn't know whether to cry or be angry? To fold or fight? But either way, all I could see in my mind's eye was Mark's smug face—the 'boutique ponce'—smarming his way between us, to soil my Marianna's purity and perfection.

But I had to be sure, be certain of my suspicions, because if I couldn't have her, then no one else sure as hell would.

Chapter Eleven

An Intruder Awaits Without

AN UNSHAKABLE PANIC SET IN, a panic that years of assured living had left me woefully ill-equipped to deal with.

I needed to know, know if her eyes had left me and strayed to one less deserving.

That question hovered around my inflating insecurity like a petulant wasp, impossible to ignore—I needed a way to find out.

I spent the morning pacing the house, trying but failing to distract my mind with increasingly mundane replication of everyday living. Acting as if nothing was out of place, in the hope that the feeling I'd been kicked in the stomach would pass.

But nothing I could do did anything to alleviate the feeling of doom saturating my self-doubt. I needed to get out of the house and distract myself— somehow.

I drove into town to take a walk around the park and treat myself to a cup of tea and a slice off carrot cake at the small, French-style cafe by the band-stand.

I took a pad and pencil with me, to sketch some ideas I'd had for a new type of puppet, to help take my mind off my worries.

I carried my tea and plate to a table outside overlooking the lake, at least, everyone referred to it as 'The Lake', but to me, it was more like a large pond.

I sat pondering what constitutes a lake—when does a pond 'become' a lake? Is it its width, length, depth?

I opened my pad and took a sip of my tea. Then settled and began sketching my ideas, ideas I'd had for a brand-new method of puppet manipulation.

Half an hour of work in and I'd polished off the mug of tea but hadn't even started on the cake yet, too engrossed in what I was doing. The distraction was working and welcome.

A girl walked by with a tray of crockery. "Can I take that for you?" she asked, nodding a look to the empty mug.

"Um? Oh yeah. Thank you. Actually, do I have to go inside to get another one?" I asked.

"I can bring one out to you, if you like, and you can pay after?"

"Really?" I said. "That would be great, thank you."

"Tea was it?" she asked. I nodded. "Shan't be a minute," she said—airily, gathering up my mug and setting off again.

I resumed my drawing.

The sun gradually burned the clouds away and began warming the ground, but there was a lovely cool breeze to freshen the air.

"Hello, lonesome," said a voice on my left shoulder.

I turned to look up at whose it was, but the sun was behind them and blinded me.

I repositioned my head so their body masked the glare.

A face gradually resolved in the umbrella of the silhouette. It was Kirsty, smiling down at me, a cup and saucer in hand.

"Ohhh, hiya," I said, with genuine surprise in my voice, "how are you?"

"I'm very well, thank you. Here alone?" she asked, looking around.

"Oh. Yeah, just me. I'm just having some tea."

She glanced down at my sketches. "Are you working?"

I shrugged dismissively. "Kind of, but not really. I'm just doing some designing, trying to work out a new way of controlling my puppets."

"That sounds interesting," she said—hovering. "I can leave you alone if you like," she added, stepping back away from the table.

"Oh. No, not at all."

"Would you mind if I joined you? Just for a bit?" she said, stepping in, hesitantly.

"Oh, God, yes. *Please*, of *course*," I insisted, clearing a space for her to sit.

She smiled and sat, shuffling her chair closer to the table. "I've never seen you down here before."

"I don't come here that often," I replied, "but if I need a break from work, I sometimes do."

"Same here," she said, "I love my little shop, but you do sometimes need a break from the same four walls, don't you?"

"Absolutely," I agreed.

"I've got my niece over helping me today. It's good experience for her, and it's a bit of money for her to go out and have some fun with. So I thought, while she's there I'd take the opportunity to pop out and have a bit of a break." She took a sip of her tea. "Is that carrot cake?" she asked, with a lift of her chin.

"Oh. Yeah, do you like carrot cake?"

"Do I?" she enthused, with roll of her big, chestnut eyes. "I was tempted to get a slice myself, but I managed to resist. Part of me wishes I hadn't now."

I slid the cake across to her and handed her a fork folded in a napkin. "I've not touched it yet. Please. I'll get myself another one."

"Noooooo. Don't be daft," she responded, lifting a halting hand and placing it against mine.

"Please. I insist," I said, with a smile.

She shrugged coyly and smiled gratefully. "Are you sure?"

"Of course, I'm sure; it's yours."

"Awe. Thank you, Sammy," she mewed, with a click of her tongue—as I rose to make my way inside and secure a replacement.

I carried the new slice of cake to the table, and Kirsty gazed up at me as I sat back down.

"You didn't have to do that," she said.

"Yes, I did. It's my pleasure," I assured her. I smiled across at her as I shuffled to get comfortable. She flushed red. "Don't wait for me, tuck in," I said.

She did. I joined her.

"Oh, the girl dropped that off while you were gone," she told me, as she pointed her fork to a fresh mug of tea sat steaming on the side.

"Ah. Good. Thanks," I said.

We ate our cakes, sharing a strangely comfortable silence in the breeze and the radiance of the sun.

Kirsty finished hers first and slid the plate away. "That was lovely, thank you."

"No problem," I said, "it's nice, isn't it?"

She beamed at me and nodded, then turned her eyes back to the table.

She began hopping her chair around until she was sat right next to me, her shoulder leaning against mine.

She looped her arm through mine and gave it a squeeze.

"So, explain to me what your idea is. How does it work?"

I admit, I was slightly taken aback by her close proximity, and I couldn't quite work out 'why' she was being so nice to me.

"It's, 'em—it's a new way of control I've thought of."

"Go on," she said, scanning my sketches with interest.

"Well. Marionettes—traditionally—use a pull and release systems, that's what the string is. But *ideally*, you'd want a push-pull way of controlling everything. It makes the manipulation more definite, not so vague, like using a string naturally is."

She craned her neck towards me to see better.

"And this is what you're sketching here?"

"Yes, exactly."

She continued studying what I'd drawn, her face just inches from my own.

I watched her as she absorbed my work. Her large, chocolate-brown eyes and long black lashes flitting as she studied the details.

The breeze carried her scent across my face, and I confess, the whole experience gave me a flutter in the pit of my stomach like I'd swallowed a bag of moths.

It's a hard thing to explain to those who weren't there, but Kirsty Green was—in our schooling days—one of the incredibly cool and beautiful girls, 'The Goddesses', just like Marianna was, and all the boys hankered for her attention.

And there she was, just inches from me, leaning her body against mine and squeezing my arm, admiring 'my' designs.

I stared at the side of her face, never having been this close to her for any length of time before.

Her skin was smooth and without blemish, and her lip-line sharp and defined. She was far more attractive than I'd ever realised before, and I couldn't take my eyes off her.

She scooped her hair elegantly behind her ear with delicate fingers and turned to look at me. "They're wonderful," she said, her face glowing with wonderment.

She seemed to find mirth in catching me watching at her.

"Oh—s-sorry," I said, turning my eyes away.

She laughed. "That's all right," she said, giving me a pally nudge with her shoulder.

"You're a talented sod, you know that," she added, turning back to my diagrams. "So what are these?" she asked, pointing to one of the details. "Are those rods? What do *they* do?"

I was impressed that she could understand my diagrams. "Well, there's *two* of them, working in parallel, to control the gross body moves, and each one has a series of concentric tubes running their length, that transfer movements from the control-handle at the top, directly to the limbs of the puppet below."

"Wow," she said, smiling at me again, "so intricate." Her eyes shone with genuine interest.

She shuffled her chair back to her original position, but I found myself not wanting her to.

I wasn't sure 'just' why she was being so nice to me, but I was enjoying the attention all the same. It took my mind off what was happening at home.

Then it dawned on me, maybe 'that' was it. Maybe Kirsty 'knew' of Marianna's infidelity, and that's 'why' she was being so nice, because she felt, in some way, sorry for me?

It seemed to fit as a theory, and part of me didn't really want her pity. But part of me also appreciated that she '*was*' being kind towards me, whatever the reason for that kindness may have been.

"So are you going to *make* one of these, to test it out?" she asked.

"Yes, I will—eventually," I replied. "Hey, maybe *you* could choose what I make to test it out? You know, I give you two options to choose from, and you pick the one you like."

"Really?" she responded, looking genuinely honoured to be asked. "I'd like that. Go on then, what are the options?"

Her eyes sparkled like diamonds at the notion, and she looked to me with a childlike expectation.

"Okay. Well. I suppose, one could be, say, a wizard? Something Tolkien-esque, long-limbed and elegant, wielding a staff of power. And the other one—maybeeee, a witch? Crony-ish, hunched and bony, with a besom-broom she uses to ride the skies at night. Maybe she could be *on* it, flying. I've never made a flying marionette before."

An image of my mother, sweeping floors, flashed briefly into my thoughts.

Kirsty became animated. "Ooooo I love witches and wizards, magic and all of that." She rolled her eyes to the sky. "Ermmmmm? The witch."

"All right. That's it then. Witch it is."

She beamed at me again, clapping joyfully like an exited child.

I watched on her happy demeanour as it filled the table.

I smiled at the sight. *You're beautiful*, I thought to myself, lost in my gazes in her direction.

Her outer brows sank, and she tilted a lilting look my way. "Oh, Sam, what a lovely thing to say. Thank you."

Shhhhhit! I thought, I'd said that out loud. I was mortified.

But she took it, without issue or embarrassment and didn't make a scene.

"Aren't you lovely?" she said, with a twee shrug. "Hey, if Mari ever doesn't want you any more, you come and see me," she said—blithely. "I could do with a man like you in my life."

Boom, there it was. So she 'did' know. Marianna '*had*' confided in her. She 'must' have done.

"Sam?" she said, with question in her voice. "I was thinking. Do you ever make marionettes of other people, *for* other people—you know—in their likeness, if they asked you to and paid you for it? The exact same way you've made the ones of yourself and Marianna that I saw in your workshop?"

The question threw me a little. "Em. I suppose I could, no one's ever asked me before. Who would it be of?"

She turned vermillion. "Well, it probably sounds narcissistic, but it would be for me, *of* me. I guess, I'd just like a three-dimensional reminder of how I look now, before I eventually lose what looks I have," she joked.

I rolled my head, examining her face. "You won't lose your looks. You'll always be attractive," I explained.

I began pointing to features on her face. "You have a sharp but full bone structure. You're not reliant on fat to round off your features to give you a youthful look. So you'll always look good and in all probability, age really well."

She stared across at me, lips parted, brows raised. "Remind me to sit with you again. You certainly know how to lift a girl's spirits."

"Oh, well. It's *just* a fact."

"Well, I *like* those types of fact." She smiled wide. "So, go on. How much would it cost, to get a puppet made?"

"Of you? Nothing," I replied, "and maybe—thinking about it—*that* could be the first puppet I make that uses my new system of control?"

"Really!" she said, looking honoured at the proposition. "Bu—surely, I'd have to pay *something* for your time and trouble."

"Nope. No, you wouldn't. It would be my pleasure, when I get a bit of down time."

Her shoulders wilted, and she melted a buttery smile across at me. "Well, okay. If you're sure," she said, with an exaggerated blink.

I liked that she was being kind to me; it felt nice, despite it being—in all probability—because she knew something of Marianna's sins.

But it felt good, and I appreciated her efforts.

She glanced down at her watch and erupted from the conversation. "God. Look at the time. I'd better get back."

She gathered her things together and stood, then stepped forwards and lowered a kiss onto my cheek. I twisted my face to accept it.

"Lovely to see you again, Sam. And if you're ever coming down here again, give me a call, and I'll see if I can get away for a bit to join you. Unless you wanted to be alone of course."

I gazed up at her lovely features, backlit by the sun and nodded. I couldn't believe it. Kirsty Green would like to meet up with '*me*', 'again'.

It felt amazing. Even if it 'was', in reality, driven by a certain amount of pity.

"Okay, I will. I'd like that."

"Me too," she said softly. "Well. Bye then."

She backed away, turned and left.

I watched her walking away, finally getting a good look at her.

She had on an optimistic, yellow summer dress, that billowed around her long, slender legs as they carried her off.

She turned and looked back at me, a coy but coquettish look on her face. "Bye," she mouthed.

I nodded and smiled. "Bye."

Six o'clock finally arrived. The day had passed as a year.

I sat at a window seat in 'Bar-Zero'—a trendy pub-restaurant situated across the road from the salon.

I ordered a bottle of beer and just enough food to prevent me looking out of place—and watched.

The girls began leaving the salon in drabs, each time, accompanied to the door by Mark and his slimy demeanour, until no one was left but him, and of course, Marianna.

I pretended to pick at the food, but I had no appetite for anything, except to witness for myself what I already knew—however unpalatable 'that' particular dish was to digest.

I couldn't help but wonder why the sympathetic magic was failing and so completely.

I figured—her discovery of it, and the subsequent knowledge of 'what' it was, and 'that' it was, had removed much, if not all of its power.

Mark appeared in the shop window, looking furtively through the glass of the door, peering either way up the high-street.

If he was in any way attempting to 'not' look suspicious, he failed in every way imaginable.

He turned the keys in the lock and twisted the blinds shut.

His shadow left the window, and the lights inside began shutting off one at a time, until just the faintest of glows remained behind the slatted shades.

My pessimistic thoughts fired into overdrive—visions of Marianna, draped over one of the salon chairs like an un-reluctant whore, offering all she had, and was, to that boutique-ponce began incinerating my imagination.

I attempted to question my suspicions, but however hard I tried, they remained relentlessly negative.

Another vision manifested—of her, bent over, leant on one of the sinks, pencil skirt rucked up around her tight little waist, and that a-sexual tosser fucking what was mine.

Hopelessly fatalistic visions flashing with all the force of Eta Carinae into my thoughts, crushing any hopes I had that I might be wrong to powder.

My throat suddenly flooded with bile, and vomit filled my mouth.

I wretched it into my napkin and scuttled my embarrassment from the bar to a fanfare of repulsed mutterings, clapping and restrained laughter.

I heaved what remained into a nearby shop doorway—thoughts that it was all over wringing my innards in its cruel, ridiculing grasp.

But 'could' I be wrong? Maybe she 'was' being trained. I had no way of knowing.

I realised that my mind, in its backfoot state, was incapable of making a judgment based on my suspicions alone. I would need hard evidence to be sure and to be fair—both to her and more importantly, me.

The next two weeks passed—me, straining every fetlock to act calm and normal, Marianna, carrying on the masquerade that she 'was' being trained.

I continued to shadow the salon, every Tuesday and Thursday.

I inspected her clothes for scents not her own and regularly checked her phone. But I learned nothing more than I'd gleaned from that first night.

Then, something different happened.

It was Thursday, and I'd followed her to the salon as usual.

136

It was raining heavily, and the sky looked decidedly thunderous, so I parked up across the street to watch, fairly certain that—hidden by the veil of inclement weather—I wouldn't be seen.

But instead of the usual routine of suspicious looks, locked doors, shutting blinds, and half of the lights turning off. This time—'all' of the lights extinguished, and the salon fell into total darkness.

I watched and waited, but no one exited the door.

I wondered what might be going on, 'why' things were different this time.

To my mind, fucking in the dark was never really a viable option when the focus of your efforts looked as good as Marianna. That just wasn't possible, was it?

Then I had a thought—Mark parked his car around the back of the store, what if they were leaving, together, through the back exit?

I quickly started my engine and pulled away—turning down the one-way street that passed the parking area at the rear to take a look.

And there they were—running from the back door of the building, chased by the rain—scurrying like excited children across the parking lot to his waiting Jaguar.

Their arms were linked, and they were laughing. It felt like they were laughing at me.

I quickly drove past, fairly certain I hadn't been seen.

I pulled up around the corner, switched off my lights and waited for them to drive past.

Eventually, they did, and I pulled out to follow them.

My mind swirled with questions: where the fuck were they going together? What possible training could they be doing away from the salon? Were my suspicions justified? Were they about to be confirmed, dashing what little remained of my self-respect on the rocks of truth?

I followed them at a safe distance, watching his tail lights shimmer through the mottling film of water running down the screen—the whir of the wipers relentless in their efforts to clear the view.

I felt sick. Part of me contemplated turning back and pretending I'd seen nothing, in the vain hope that it might all just go away.

But the other part for me saw through that baseless wish, so I carried on following.

Eventually—they turned into the parking lot of 'Tricolour', an intimate French restaurant sat midway between Bradlington and the neighbouring town.

It was a favourite haunt for those of wealth and fashion and boasted a Michelin-star, which made the inbred yokels in the area cream with pride that they had something a little bit 'London' near-by.

I drove past, parked up and watched them hurry from his car and dart inside. Again, they were holding hands.

The gut-punch feeling returned. I could hardly draw breath. Twenty years of work and happiness was crumbling around me, and I had no answers.

I rose from the car and ambled through the relentless curtains of incessant rain towards a truth I wasn't sure I could handle. We three, me, Marianna and that nail in my coffin—Mark, could have been the only people on earth for all the attention I was capable of giving to the rest of the world.

It was a weekday, so the surrounding area was relatively quiet. Apart from the sodden hiss of the occasional passing motorist, I was the only person around.

I stooped to peek through each waist-level window of the seventeenth century building, seeking a glimpse of the traitors.

Then I found them, being shown to a table opposite window number four.

A girl escorted them, removing a reserved sign from the table as they took to their seats. But oddly, neither of them was looking around at the restaurant's decor. Had they been here before? Together?

I was almost certain—given his type—that Mark must 'surely' have frequented this place.

But Marianna? Why wasn't 'she' checking it out? 'We' sure as hell hadn't been there together. But had 'she' been there before—'without' me? With 'him'?

They looked at their menus, but Mark kept flicking glances her way. But who can blame him, he was sat opposite a specimen of nature's finest work. A woman so beautiful I had devoted my life to securing her affections.

Boutique-ponce or not, he was still a man.

The girl arrived cradling a bottle of wine, showed the label to Mark and poured him a little.

He sipped at it like a connoisseur, nodded knowledgeably, and the girl charged their glasses.

They gave their orders, or at least 'he' did, for the both of them—playing the smarmy gent to a tee.

The waitress left with their orders, and they raised their glasses to toast something or other? Was it to celebrate their infidelity? I just watched it all unfold through the veil of rain.

I contemplated running inside and confronting them and making a scene. But that wasn't my way and would've been beneath me. I just needed to observe them interact, watch them together and in so doing—glean a truth that a large part of me would rather not have known.

I moved in closer to the window, rain pouring off my hair.

They began talking, or at least 'he' did, Mari just listened.

She seemed transfixed by him. Sort of fascinated, fascinated by his words, his ways, like he had some sort of spell on her. The irony cut into me like a scalpel.

Then he said something, something that made her react.

She tilted her head to one side, her face a picture of pleasant surprise, or was it shocked appreciation showing on her face? She appeared somewhat flattered?

Then her whole face gaped, then morphed into a smile. She hung in a look of shock, then mouthed the words 'no way'?

They both leaned into each other, deeper into the conversation, their faces now just inches apart.

What the fuck could he have been saying to arrest her interest 'that' fucking much?

I couldn't stand it—just hovering there like a moron, watching. Secretly observing that wanker stealing away my dreams, my life. And me just looking on like a spineless idiot.

But physically, he was much bigger than me. Built. One of those gym types that could've snapped me like a dry twig, and I simply didn't have the nerve to go inside and say something.

So I slinked away, drove home and left them to their underhand dalliance.

But, by then, I was sure of one thing and one thing alone. She 'was' having an affair, and if 'I' wasn't to have her, then no one else sure as hell was going to.

I knew then—I would kill her, and him, and feel entirely justified in my decision to do so.

She had turned from the food of my happiness, to the fuel for my misery, and the bitterness that was boiling inside of me would power my ability to wipe her from the face of the earth and do so in the most despicable way I could muster.

And him? Well. His death would be painful, as painful as any death could possibly be.

A gift—from me to him—for daring to take what was rightfully mine. What I'd fought to win and promised to care for, for two decades of my life.

If he believed in any way, that I would simply stand by and watch him stroll in and steal away that that was mine—without recourse or retribution—then he was 'sorely' mistaken.

The following week felt decidedly awkward. Not an awkwardness 'between' us, just an awkwardness for me, having to fight to not display what I knew.

But I had to keep up the pretence that I was clueless to their infidelity. There were things I needed to do before I could dispense with them both, things that would be far easier to accomplish with them believing I knew nothing of their assignations.

Fact is, in the same way that there are a thousand ways to crack an egg, there are a thousand ways you can extinguish a life using the occult. And the method I'd devised to dispatch those traitorous fucks put me right at the centre of the mode of their murder.

An amalgamation of techniques that would ultimately give me back the control I'd lost and craved. A method that would rid me of the anger that was eating me alive.

But first—I needed an effigy of Mark. But not a poppet this time, my chosen method required a 'puppet'.

Having a photographic memory, it would be a reasonably simple task for me to carve a marionette of that backstabbing wanker, and I did have the pictures from the garden party as reference.

But in order to complete it, I would need five things: some of his hair, his clothing, his saliva, his blood. And of course, his astrological details.

For whatever reason, my book of shadows had no mention of him anywhere within its pages. Had this thing been going on for longer than I first thought? Why hadn't I ever met him before any of this?

I worked on crafting the marionette of Mark for most of that week. It would be the tool I would use to orchestrate his end, and likewise, the marionette of Marianna would be key to manipulating 'her' sorry demise.

The puppets would be the controllers, 'the transmitters', the beacons as it were, ethereally linked to each one of them, and as the puppets do, so do they— so mote it be.

I also decided—against my better instincts and judgment—to once again call on the services of Aishma, my most utilised of all the demons of Hell. To oversee the implementation of my will and to lend his own peculiar brand of cruelty to the proceedings, to make certain its success. I figured—why hit a butterfly with a newspaper, when there's a hammer to hand.

It took me four days to complete the puppet of Mark. Four gruelling days of pretence and forced ignorance to the fact that my Marianna was at the salon, being fucked like the whore that she'd become by this plucked and preened, linen jacket adorning, pretentious asshole.

God, I could taste my desire to kill him coating the back of my throat—the increasingly frequent thoughts of them together making the whole undertaking a laughably easy proposition to comprehend. I simply couldn't wait.

But—I'd have to. I needed those five things, and their acquisition was next on my agenda.

Chapter Twelve

Blood, Sweat, Tears

IT FELT NOTHING LIKE SO LONG, but more than two months had passed since Marianna had found the draw. The weather had stepped across the divide and could no longer be considered summery.

Sure, there were occasional hot days, but they'd become fewer—less frequent—and heavy rain and cold climes had become the more common of the sky's offerings.

The trees that surrounded the cottage had begun to brown, painting the backdrop of my upward gazes with copper and gold.

But none of that mattered, none of 'any' of it mattered. All I could think of—was 'kill them'.

Resentment had taken up permanent residence in my resolve, and the passage of time only transpired to make it bitter.

It was a Tuesday morning. I was in the kitchen.

Marianna was upstairs getting ready for work—as usual—then she trotted down the staircase and flawed me with a landmine of a revelation.

"So—honey—I forgot to tell you last night," she chirped, "Mark has asked me to go away with him, to a hair and beauty event in Coventry. It's a convention—you know the sort of thing. 'He' goes every year, but this time, he'd like me to go with him."

I physically gasped, but she didn't even seem to notice, she just carried on.

"I said yes of course, well—you have to show willing. But apparently, there's stuff happening over at the salon that he doesn't want to jinx by talking about yet, but he says it'd be good for me to go and learn a bit more about all aspects of the styling business. So I thought—why not, so I said, yes."

She blurbed this bullshit so brightly, so airily, I almost believed her—'Almost'.

My mind mumbled and froze. I felt numb. "W-W-What? You're going away?" I asked. My jaw felt as if it was resting on the ground.

"Ohhhh, not for ages yet, it's a couple of weeks away at least. And I'll only be away for a night, or possibly two? It's a two-day event, so I'm not quite sure, but I'll ask him."

I could say nothing, stunned by the sheer ease of it all.

I hardly recognised her anymore. a goddess for sure, but a goddess with no heart—at least, not for me.

"Listen," she piped, "I have to dash. I'm running late, but remember, it's my training night tonight, so don't wait up for me, okay?"

I had a sudden thought come to mind—an idea—and the opportunity and the timing felt right. "Oh, well in that case, I have a marionette I need to drop off to a client, so maybe I could do 'that' this evening, if you're going to be away?" I suggested. Of course, it was bullshit, but by then, I had little problem feeding it to her. "The guy's been away and won't be back until later this evening. But I could drive over and drop it off then. What do you think?"

She threaded her arm through the strap of her tote bag and turned to me nodding. "Yeah. Sure. That sounds good to me." She smiled, raising her brows theatrically. "Another job, huh, aren't you doing well? My clever little puppet maker," she sang, in what could possibly be taken as a slightly condescending tone. Or again—not?

She leaned her perfect red lips in towards me and pressed them up against mine. My eyes rolled as the taste of her breath infused my mouth.

She hung in the kiss, pressing it into what remained of my desire for her attention—twisting her soft mouth a quarter turn, lapping her tongue beneath mine and up against the inside of my cheek.

She drew back and cupped her hand to my face—looking me straight in the eyes.

She smiled warmly into my elated gaze. "I'm proud of you, you know that," she said, softly—stroking her thumb tenderly across my cheek. "I love you, Sam," she added, looking somehow remorseful, almost guilty?

Then with a giggle, she wiped my lips clear of the vibrant crimson left by her almost believable show of affection, then straightened to leave.

I was confused. It felt every bit like she meant it. Was she 'that' good of a liar?

"Okay. Got-ta-go," she choired, with another of her heart-crushing smiles that sang from her eyes as much as the lips—pecking a parting kiss on the end of my nose.

She gathered her things together, then left through the door.

I slumped into the chair and contemplated my scrambled feelings.

The kiss, I was sure it felt real—'meant'—and not delivered with just enough compassion to delay the need to confront a problem with a dying relationship. A very 'real' kiss, erotic even.

Or was I just allowing myself to be sucked into her lies and deceit? To be deluded by her actions and my own desires. 'So' hankering for more of that kind of attention from the Aphrodite in my life, that I sought a truth—however erroneous—that simply fitted a narrative that suited my wants?

A spine-petrifying scream suddenly pierced the air. It came from somewhere outside, and the tone of the voice that produced it, sounded like Marianna?

I jumped up from the table and ran outside.

Marianna's car was still parked in the driveway—engine running, driver's door open.

She was walking backwards up the drive, faced away from me, her body hunched over, one hand clutching her stomach, the other clasped across her mouth.

She continued to back towards me, visibly shaken by something? She didn't seem to realise I'd emerged.

"What's the matter?" I asked.

She yelped and spun to face me, looking at me as though I was a stranger. "What is it?" I reiterated. "What's happened?"

She started to back away from me, extending her arm towards the garage, pointing a needle-straight finger. "W-Why would you do that?" she asked, in a strained, mute tone—her voice shaking.

"Do what? What's happened?"

She stiffened her pointing arm. "In there, I found a—a b-bin bag, with a d-dead dog in it. Why would you do that?"

My stomach folded. I'd forgotten all about that fucking dog.

I'd meant to dispose of it long before, but with everything that was going on around me—I'd forgotten.

"Oh, Jesus Christ!" I slurred—despairing—trying to think fast on my feet. "I found it in the road, it'd been hit, I think by a car, or a lorry, or something, but I didn't want the owner to find it like that, so I put it in a bag and was going to ask around—you know—to find out who owned it. But I forgot. I've been so busy, I forgot. I'm so sorry."

She ceased backing away, her body turned three-quarters on from me, postured as though readying herself to sprint.

The slightly distrusting look in her eyes remained. The exact same look she'd destroyed me with by the sink when she thrust the doll out towards me, on the day it all went to shit.

I lifted my arms out towards her, tilting my head and took a gentle step towards her. "I'm sorry. I'm so, so sorry you had to find that, Mari. I just forgot—okay? Please forgive me. I was only trying to do the right thing."

She seemed to mortify slightly at my approach, still obviously swimming in her repulsion at what she'd found.

It had been there days, weeks even, just rotting.

I stepped in and wrapped my arms around her and kissed the side of her head.

She was shaking in my embrace. "My apologies, I'm sorry. I'll deal with it today, okay? I promise. I'm sorry."

She nodded quietly in my arms. "Come on," I said, leading her to her car. "Get yourself off to work, you're going to be late. I'll deal with it *right* now. Don't worry."

She took a long, slow breath. "Okay," she mumbled, sounding apologetic.

She turned to me. "It was just the shock—you know—at finding it there. I didn't mean to over react."

I smiled at her. "You *didn't* over react—you reacted. The same way I probably would if I found something like that. So don't worry about it. It was *my* mistake."

The distrust seemed to have drained from her demeanour. But had it really?

She lifted her face from her humbled gait and gave me an impassionate peck on the mouth. Then lowered herself into her car again, backed up and drove away.

I seethed at myself. "You stupid fucking idiot!" I gnashed through gritted teeth.

But why? What did I even care? I wasn't supposed to give a shit anymore. I was going to kill the cheating bitch and that asshole lover of hers. 'And' she'd only just fed me some crap about a hair-and-beauty convention that I instinctively knew didn't even exist.

A vision of the two of them, together, flashed my thoughts, and the blood-boiling hatred returned. The hatred that would ease the path to killing them.

The day rolled by, and darkness fell, blanketing the countryside with a cold calmness that felt good to stand in.

An evening dew lifted the pine scents of the surrounding trees into the air, and I stood on the patio in the core of the musk, breathing it in.

I checked the time on my phone. 19:12—I needed to leave, there were things I needed to do.

I went back inside and dropped into the basement.

I grabbed the Temazepam off the shelf, shook a few of the tablets into my hand and with a pestle and mortar, ground them into a fine dust.

I folded the powder it into a torn-off slither of paper and pocketed it.

I slipped on my dark hoody—grabbing a selection of screwdrivers, a pair of scissors, a syringe and needle, a few zip-lock bags and a knife and pocketed them also.

I locked the house and set off.

I sat in the car around the corner from the salon parking area, waiting for Mark to drive past.

I didn't have to wait long—I'd timed it perfectly.

After less than half-an-hour, his Jaguar hoovered by, and to my relief, Marianna wasn't with him.

I gently pulled out and followed him.

After about an eighteen-minute drive, he turned in through some wrought-iron gates and parked up outside of a detached Victorian house.

It was somewhat more modest and much more 'normal' than I'd imagined it would be, but still, I had to admit—a very nice place.

I quickly parked up on the street outside, quietly nudging my door shut with my hip, then darted through the gates as he let himself through the front door.

He shouted out to what I assumed was some form of animal. "Molly" he called, which made me think it was probably a cat.

An absence of barking, and his calls proving fruitless in raising any form of warm welcome, I was certain it must be something feline.

I quietly and quickly ran down the side-passage into the back-garden, just as the lights flashed on.

I ducked down behind a brick-built barbecue and watched as he pottered about the kitchen.

He poured himself a glass of red wine and began preparing some brand of pasta dish. Tomatoes, bell peppers, and I think, penne pasta?

A cat—that I presumed must be Molly—approached the inside of the patio doors that opened out into the garden.

It slinked up to the cat flap and hesitated, then began turning looks in Mark's direction. Obnoxiously pompous looks on its stupid, privileged face.

"What?" Mark said—feigning agitation. "Oh, go on then. Lady muck," he called—jokingly, rounding the kitchen counter to let the cat through the door. "You use the cat flap when I'm not here, so I don't understand why you insist I have to let you out when I *am*. Awkward bugger," he complained—but lovingly.

But if it were down to me, I'd have shoved the smug little bastard through the flap.

He swung the door open, and the cat stepped cautiously out into the night, sniffing the dew-scented air.

I shrunk back behind the wall. Then I had a thought, *What if this damned animal senses me, smells me and draws attention to my presence here?*

Mark stood at the door watching the mog stepping gingerly into the night, striding hesitantly in my direction. *Fuck?* I thought, If he 'did' discover me, what would I do—apart from run and hope the ponce was too muscle bound to follow.

Just as I was about to spill over into panic mode, the house phone rang out, and Mark left the open door to answer it.

I slumped, breathed, then grabbed my chance and rose from my hiding place.

The cat howled like a siren, leapt four feet off the ground and scampered from the garden.

I poked my head through the patio doors, pulling the hood back from my ear to listen.

I could hear Mark's voice, muffled by distance, talking to someone he seemed happy to hear from. Could it have been Marianna?

He seemed to be in what I imagined must've been the living room, at least two rooms away at the front of the house.

I stepped tentatively inside and scanned the kitchen. There were two possibilities open to me that I could see: the pan of ragu which was sitting ready on the hob, the heat turned off. Or his glass of wine.

I opted for the ragu—far more volume to hide any taste.

I drew the paper wrap carefully from my pocket, unfolded it and tapped the Temazepam into the saucepan.

My finger caught the corner of the paper, flicking some of the powder onto the black, glass surface of the hob. "Shit!" I spat, under my voice.

I quickly began scooping up the dust with the side of my thumb, flicking it into the pan with my fingers.

I darted a look down the corridor and paused for a moment. I could still hear him speaking, he sounded mid-conversation and in no hurry to finish—at least I hoped that was the case.

I had to get out of there before he returned. What would I do if he did? I darted a look at the chef's knife lying on the chopping board. If he 'did' discover me, I'd have to kill him—there and then—and that was just 'not' part of my plan.

I finally managed to clear away the spillage, and quickly stirred the Temazepam into the sauce.

I turned, and cocked an ear towards the hallway. Mark was still mid-call, the conversation flowing like a river.

My eyes caught sight of a bunch of keys lying on the counter in front of me. There was one brass key—a Yale type—separated from the cluster. I guessed it must have been the key to the front door, the one he'd been holding when he let himself in.

I quickly wound it off the ring, and slipped it into my pocket.

I placed the keys back roughly the way they were, and slid out through the patio doors again.

Mark eventually returned. I settled at the back of the garden on an upturned plant pot behind a shrub, and waited.

Watching the boutique-ponce milling about his kitchen was somehow hypnotic—soothing—and apart from it getting cold, and the discomfort of the make-shift seat, I could have sat there for hours, simply watching him living his life. Finding interest in both the similarities, and the differences to the way he and I did things.

Similarities seemed to win outright, maybe there were only a handful of ways to crack an egg?

He sat down at a sort of breakfast bar tagged onto the end of his preparation area, and began eating—opening his post as he chewed.

I stood back in the shadows, watching him through the kitchen window.

He ate all of the pasta, mopping up the remnants of the sauce with a few slices of focaccia. Then he stood, carried his plate to the sink and filed it away with the rest of the dirty dishes crowding the basin.

His expression suddenly began to muddy, stretching his face long, widening his eyes and he started to become unsteady on his feet.

He peered at his wine glass like he didn't know what it was and clacked it down on the counter.

It was a look I'd seen many times before in Marianna's face, and over time, she'd ended up harbouring a belief that she simply wasn't good with alcohol.

Mark stumbled from the kitchen and weaved down the hallway, walking the walls with his hands and staggered to the front room.

I quickly made my way down the side-passage to the bay-window at the front and continued to observe him succumbing to the Temazepam.

He staggered backwards and slumped lengthways onto the sofa, reaching out his arm to fumble for the remote control. But he swiped it onto the floor and passed out.

I waited a good fifteen minutes to make certain Mark was fully under the influence of the Temazepam, then took the key from my pocket and approached the front door.

But then I remembered—he'd never got around to locking the back door.

I made my way back around to the patio and quietly slipped inside.

I carefully threaded the key back onto the fob, then made my way along the hallway towards the living room.

I passed one door leading to a room with a single window, filled to the rafters with gym equipment.

The decor further inside was at odds to the relative modernness of the kitchen area. More traditionally Victorian and in keeping with the architecture of the house: tiled floors and stain-glass panels. Elaborate but imposing furniture, French in style and painted to look weathered—a popular trend at that time, especially among the members of the populace devoid of an original thought or idea of their own.

I could hear the heaviness of his breathing as I neared the door to the living room.

I began drawing what I needed from my pockets: the syringe, scissors, sample pot, zip-lock bag.

I cautiously rounded the doorframe. He was still sprawled out in exactly the same position he had been a few minutes earlier.

I turned a look towards the window. If 'I' was able to see in from the outside, then others could too.

I tiptoed over and quietly pulled the curtains shut, glancing over my shoulder to check the metallic brush of the rings hadn't woken him.

His arm was still hanging off the edge of the seat, the pit of his elbow facing the ceiling—a fortuitous stroke of luck indeed.

I knelt down beside him and gently brushed his arm to see if he would stir. He didn't, he was out cold. but I 'had' given him 50mg.

I unsheathed the needle and carefully presented it to a worm of a vein running along his muscular forearm. Gingerly, and with a wince—I pushed it in.

He broke from his slumber and stirred, and it took all my strength to hold his muscular arm fast and prevent him from folding it on his chest, potentially snapping the needle in his arm.

My unblinking eyes burned his flickering lids, expecting them to open and look straight at me. But they remained shut, until finally, he settled back into a torpor again.

I took a full breath. And breathed it out slowly—attempting to pacify the squirrel that was charging around my guts.

A bead of saliva began to run from the corner of his mouth. I quickly grabbed my chance and the sample pot from my pocket and gently scooped it up.

I replaced the lid and pocketed it.

I pulled the plunger on the syringe, and the tube filled claret-red. I re-sheathed it and pocketed that too.

I snipped a few locks of hair from the top of his head; it was fairly long, so wouldn't be noticed. Then I struggled to my feet and left the room to find a few items of his clothing.

I found a wash basket in the bathroom upstairs and took a dress shirt, a t-shirt and a pair of pants from the pile.

I noticed some toenail shavings in the bathtub—a bonus item that I could utilise to create an even stronger bond—and bagged them also.

I made my way back downstairs to the living room. I could still hear him breathing heavily, rasping the occasional snore that shook the walls.

I stepped in, opened the curtains again and turned to leave. But then I noticed, there was a bead of blood dripping down his arm.

Damn it, I thought, I couldn't leave him like that, it looked exactly like what it was, and I knew finding it would raise suspicions and draw attention to the puncture wound. I had to think—and fast.

I quickly trotted down the hallway to the kitchen and took up his wine glass.

I gripped it firmly, snapping the stem, then carried it to the front room.

I dragged the clean break across the puncture wound on his arm, and it began to bleed, profusely enough to mask my intrusion.

He didn't stir, by that time, the Temazepam had him fully under its spell.

I dabbed my thumb in the blood and rubbed some onto 'his' fingers. Then I took the broken glass back to the kitchen and posed it on the worktop, pouring a little of the wine from the half empty bottle around it, my hope being that he would think he somehow cut himself in his apparent drunken stupor. But only time would out on that one.

I left the house with bounty secure, letting the cat back in as I did.

I drove for home, feeling satisfied, smug even, with my night's work.

I imagined I felt the same way a special forces op. would feel when flying back from a mission. A self-satisfied pride at completing a job well done. A job that ultimately, you'd 'never' be able to speak of.

Half way home—and prompted by the stench of decomposing flesh drifting forwards in the car—I pulled into a layby.

I checked the coast was clear and extricated the bagged-dog carcass from the boot and hurled it into a ditch, kicking fresh fallen leaves from autumn's efforts on top for good measure.

Back at the cottage, the lights were on, and Marianna's car was already there—parked up outside the garage.

I slipped off the hoodie and stowed it beneath my seat. It needed washing—badly—having attained a smell similar to old books and wet compost.

It was the exact same aroma my sports kit had evolved over five years of schooling, unfriended by soap or the concept of washing.

But I'd owned 'this' garment for years and had only ever worn it for short moments at a time to perform my covert tasks.

But the reality was—if you totted up all the hours I'd had it on, it would probably equate to a good couple of months straight. And the scent it was emitting sang to that fact. "Jesus," I said out loud, "it smells worse than that fucking dog."

I carefully secreted my ill-gotten gains into my socks, then spent a moment in the mirror assuring myself that my expression displayed no evidence of my knowledge that Marianna was being defiled by her boss, then exited the car and made my way inside to continue the pretence that I was clueless to the outrage, and the ungrateful whore was still getting away with it.

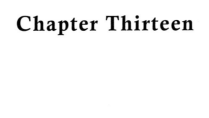

Chapter Thirteen

An Actor Prepares

BY THE TIME I GOT IN, it was late. So I quickly grabbed a bite to eat.

"Hi, Sammy," came a voice from above, like a soft call from something divinely celestial.

Marianna descended the stairs like a gliding angel, clothed in her favourite night-dress. It was pastel blue, with a large teddy bear on the front, and it gave her heart-wrenching beauty a kind of cuteness that made her irresistible.

It also clung to the peaks and troughs of that incredible body, a sure-fire distraction and made the job of pretending I knew nothing of her disloyalty just that little easier to pull off.

She walked across to join me at the table.

She stooped to deliver a kiss on my lips; I stretched up to receive it—just like I normally would.

Her breath had a minty after-taste, she must have only just brushed her teeth.

Her whole mouth tasted clean and fresh, and her lips—without the usual coating of gloss—had a texture akin to velvet, pillowing mine with a softness only female skin can possess.

The air left my body, and I felt heady and faint. The exact same sensation I'd had the very first time our mouths ever touched, all those years back when the magic had first delivered to me, that, which I'd coveted for so, so long.

She sat down before me. I couldn't take my eyes off her. Even without makeup, she was everything.

"So, how's your day been? Did you manage to see that guy and drop the puppet off?" she asked.

She seemed genuinely interested, and it all felt painfully normal, like nothing was wrong, or going on?

I had to work hard to snap out of my trance. "Erm? Oh, yeah. Yes, I did. He seemed very happy with what I'd done."

"Well, I should imagine he was. Everything you make is amazing—everybody says so. I'll never understand just how you come up with your ideas, then carve them from solid blocks of wood. It fascinates me."

I just stared at her lips as she spoke to me, moving to the sound of her angelic voice. I may very well have put a spell on 'her', but she undeniably had one on 'me'.

"Um. Yes. Practice makes perfect, I guess," I responded, feeling far removed and in my own little world.

She frowned at me quizzically and tittered, "Are you okay? You seem miles away tonight." She clicked her fingers towards my face. "Testing, testing. Calling Samuel Grant. Is there anybody in there? Come in, come in, you strange, talented brand of nincompoop."

She was being funny; I 'loved' her when she was being funny and that was dangerous—given what I had to do.

I needed motivation to continue my 'work', my 'task', to end the farce that dishonoured me.

"Sorry, love. I was just thinking about another job that might be coming in. Tell me about your training. How's that going?" Let's get her talking about Mark, that'll do it—I thought.

"My training? Actually, it's *really* interesting. I've been learning about colouring. The best methods for different types of hair. When you have to lighten hair first before dyeing it. Different methods of highlighting. Ways of correcting a bad colour job—we actually get a lot of those through the door, you know, when other salons have cocked it up."

"And when is it you're going away again? With Mark?" I asked. I needed the resentment to return, all I was feeling at that moment, was my lifelong love for her.

"Oh, that's this weekend coming, and I think we *are* actually going to be away for two nights."

"What a surprise," I mumbled under my voice. I couldn't help it.

"What's that, love?"

"I said, 'I'm not surprised', sweetheart; I'm sure there'll be much for you to see."

We continued exchanging pleasantries and stories of our day while I ate. Of course—mine were all lies, and I suspected much of hers were too.

I made us hot drinks to take up and washed my plate before locking up.

We eventually made our way upstairs to bed, and Marianna's day came to an end. But mine was only just beginning.

I'd drugged her tea, and once she'd slipped under, I drew a vial of blood from her arm, and I was set.

I descended into my workshop to finalise the work I'd been secretly doing for the past week.

I applied Mark's hair to his marionette, a painstaking process, knotting each strand onto fine mesh, then applying it onto the head I'd carved to represent him. I then stitched clothes from the garments I'd taken from his house and dressed him.

Four and a half hours of eye-straining work later, and I was adding the final, finishing touches.

Finally, I strung it, and it was done.

I lifted it to its feet and leant back, holding it on a straight arm to examine my craftsmanship.

It looked good, just like him, in fact. It had his hair, his clothes and his astrological details carved with care into the soft grains of the timber—those I'd managed to find in Marianna's diary.

All I needed to do now, was soak the fibres of the wood with his blood and link it to him, then finally, at last, he would be at my mercy.

I offered the new puppet up to the marionette of Marianna. Then it occurred to me—her name—'Marianna'. So close to the word 'Marionette' that it amazed me that I hadn't noticed the similarity before.

Was that another sign? Or was I simply seeking affirmation to justify my actions wherever the opportunity arose to see it?

But it was undeniable—as unpalatable as the reality was to digest—that these two puppets looked, somehow, right together. More so than if I'd placed the one of her, next to the one of me.

I began to weep for the reality of the situation I was in. I didn't want to lose her, but I knew I already had, and that just re-ignited the resentment in me that I knew could only be pacified by her death.

Her purity had been sullied. Defiled. Her perfection stained by the oily fingers of lust.

Outside of my mother, she was the only female I'd really ever had in my life, so it wasn't much of a stretch for me to imagine—however false that notion may have been—that I was the only boy she'd ever entertained, or loved. Or at least, she'd 'believed' she loved.

But now, unquestionably, she was a fallen angel that had let sin into her big, red heart and to my bottomless pit of despair; she needed 'cleansing'.

But the resentment I felt for her, was as nothing to that that I felt for him.

I would 'fuck' him up good and proper, for taking away what was mine. My happiness. My world. My life—my Marianna. And despite my undoubtable fears and apprehension for the idea, I would summon 'Aishma' once again, to add his particular and unnervingly peculiar brand of cruelty to the proceedings.

I would be the orchestrator, the conductor as t'were, and he would play the music and rub from my spoiled life the oily cunt who'd ruined it all.

With ardour restored, I drilled holes to the hearts of each marionette and slowly dripped the vials of blood into each of their tiny bodies, soaking the fibres of the timber with the very essence of each of them.

I burned the toenail clippings and sprinkled the ashes in there too for good measure.

A few drops to the respective mouths of the saliva I'd collected, and the making was finished.

There followed an hour of ritual at my altar and the raising the brightest cone of power I'd ever invoked. The whole roof of the house seemed to shudder when I projected it out from the house, frightening me with its sheer force, but all was complete—it was done.

I lay the puppets safely in my draw in readiness for 'the performance' of their deaths and exhausted by my night's work, I climbed the stairs to re-join Marianna in bed.

She was still out cold. I pulled her unconscious body in tight to me and held her close.

A strange kind of tranquillity inhabited me in the week that followed—the week before they were to go away together.

I weirdly came to terms with what was happening and what was 'going' to happen, and it gave me a found ability to just enjoy the best of who Marianna was for those remaining few days.

Maybe I was simply showing her the best of who 'I' was, so that she may know of what it was she'd lost as she slipped away into death.

Or maybe, I was just relishing the remaining days I had with her, the girl that for two decades was everything to me. The girl—quite literally—of my dreams.

But whatever it was, I grasped the opportunity, and we lived a week of love, lust and romance.

It was the stuff true fantasies are made of, fantasies I once had before I became part of the dream.

That following evening, we went to the cinema to see the noir-classic *Strangers on a Train*. We'd seen it before of course—it being a firm favourite of ours—but there was nothing like seeing it on the big, silver screen, and we relived the first time we ever saw it.

Then we dined together at 'La Rue', a small but personable French restaurant on the high-street.

Afterwards—we fucked in the restrooms, something we did a lot when we were younger and our love was fresh.

We were acting like teenagers again, everything feeling new, exciting, with a 'first time' quality to everything we did.

I fell in love with her all over again, but strangely, it didn't appear to effect my desire to erase her from my life for what she'd done to me.

I guess, I was simply using her. Using her to feed my physical and emotional needs—an affection prostitute if you like—and the fee for her services, was my undivided care and attention.

The days rolled by, and despite the fact that we were both in some way acting, we were happy. Or at least, we 'appeared' happy.

But no, we 'were' happy, and I guess the mechanisms that could explain just how that could've been were just too complex for me to fathom. So I didn't bother trying, I just enjoyed her.

Friday arrived. I hadn't slept much. I lay awake most of the night watching Marianna sleeping.

She had a calmness in slumber like she hadn't a care in the world, which of course—in her mind—she hadn't. But I knew otherwise.

I wondered as I watched—was she dreaming of him, or of me? Maybe neither of us. But whatever it was she dreamt, it gave her face a look as tranquil as a midnight pool on a moonless night.

She woke to the sight of me staring at her, and her eyes met mine.

Her brows winced quizzical for the briefest of moments, then she closed them, wrapped her arm around my neck and with a groan of what seemed like contentment, pulled me into her. "Morning," she whispered into my ear, like it was a secret that the night had ended.

I buried my face in her hair and curled my hand around her flawless body and caressed the flexing arch of her spine. "Morning," I replied, as she writhed in my arms.

We rolled apart, and she stretched herself long, cycling her legs to draw the duvet to the foot of the bed.

My hand gravitated to her stomach as she racked herself. She had the tightest of stomachs, flat and taut like the skin of a drum.

"God, you're beautiful," I said, softly, as my fingers fascinated over her flexing abdomen. I didn't realise I'd even said it out loud until I saw it in her face.

Her brows twisted in a kind of pitying fondness at my words. "Oh, sweetheart. What's gotten into *you* this morning?"

But I couldn't tell her. Tell her that I was savouring my final moments in her company. In less than a day, she'd be in 'his' arms, and a short time later, dead.

Would she be as relaxed with him, as she seemed to be with me? Questions I asked but that I had no interest in knowing the answers to.

But what I 'could' tell her, was what was inside of me. Inside of my heart. "I love you. I'm going to miss you," I said with sincerity, straight to her face.

Her fine, shapely brows buckled again. She looked bemused by what I'd said, then they relaxed and smoothed over.

She pursed her lips loosely, and offered them to me. They pillowed mine and she drilled their softness into my bliss.

She released and dropped her head back on the pillow, gaze locked on mine, a sentimental smile licking at the corners of her mouth and eyes.

Her intense gaze drew me in like a tractor beam. I lowered another kiss onto her welcoming mouth.

She pursed again to receive it, and I held it and held it and held it, relishing the flavour of her buttery skin on mine.

Marianna twisted out of the embrace and caught a breath, turning back to me. "Sorry, honey, I've not brushed my teeth yet," she said, with a smile and a tender stroke of my face.

But 'I' had already been up that morning, and brushed mine while I was there.

"I don't care," I muttered affectionately into her eyes. "I *want* to taste you. I *need* to taste you."

She visibly softened. The fond-pity returned to her face, and her eyes fluttered closed.

Her fingers clawed the back of my neck and dragged my head down to hers.

Our lips melded, and her mouth parted wide, exhaling a whole lungful of her saccharin breath into mine.

I felt like I was going to explode at the sensation, my heart quickening to a sprint.

The poppets, bound and stitched in the dark-drawer downstairs flashed into my mind. Their magic was strong that morning, and I was accepting of it all.

Her clawed fingers dragged me to the side, and she climbed on top of my eternal gratitude, for this and the past twenty years of moments such as these that had given my existence meaning.

Her arms crossed and lifted her night-dress clear of her softly toned torso. She slung it aside and gripped my shoulders.

The distant look in her eyes was back, and she burned it into me with flaming longing.

"I l-love you," she stuttered, as she lowered onto me.

Her eyes rolled shut and turned to the ceiling, arching her spine and gripping the backs of my knees.

I detached momentarily from what was happening. It would sometimes happen during times such as this, times that were so much greater than someone with my standing could have ever hoped to witness, let alone participate, that my mind began not to believe it real.

It felt like I was watching one of those erotic movies that I'd never gone in for. I hadn't needed to. I had perfection on my arm and nothing could ever have topped that.

But I watched, staring, gazing up at the muscles rippling up her sublimely beautiful body as she rode me.

She rose and fell and rippled before me, hypnotising my thirsty eyes until the feelings in my loins carried me back into the room—and I released.

Her stomach stretched long, then curled inwards, bringing her sweat-glazed lips back to mine, and she simpered a stuttering scream into my open mouth.

I engulfed her in my arms and caressed her for the final time, turning my mouth to her ear and whispering—"I will always love you, my dearest, incredible Marianna."

"I-I-I know," she whimpered, still shaking in my arms. "I know."

We lay as one, a singular entity, for what I knew would be the last ever time.

I rose and left her to savour the epinephrin coursing through her veins and made my way downstairs to make breakfast—her 'last supper'.

Chapter Fourteen

The Stage

THE WEIRDEST FEELING came over me as I watched her leaving for work.

I'd slipped a slither of parchment into her overnight bag before she'd left, not so much a curse, more of a beacon, guiding Aishma to them. They had been marked.

They were to set off for this alleged convention straight after work—apparently—staying the night in a hotel so they could get an early start.

It took all that existed within me to not blurt out the word 'bullshit' when she told me, and if I hadn't already made up my mind that all was lost, then I might have done.

But my tongue remained still and my voice—silent, and I acted like I'd swallowed the lot.

I guess, the weird feeling came from knowing she was never to set foot in the house ever again. 'Our' house, the home we'd built together and shared for a majority of our years.

I confess, the thought made my tear ducts empty down the regret scolding my face, and I folded inside—crushed by the enormity of the event.

Losing her, it turned out, was even more momentous than winning her affection in the first place, and I'd always considered that the pinnacle of all that was possible.

After an hour of sobbing, I rose from my kitchen floor grief-hole and washed my face clear of my emotions.

I dabbed my face dry on the towel. My lids were reddened and as sore as a loser, used only to being wet on the inside.

"Are you *sure* you're doing the right thing?" I said out loud, questioning my intentions. My ardour was softening; I was growing weak.

The washing up bowl beneath me sat half filled with water. I twisted behind me and took up the pan I'd fried the bacon in and poured some of the oil onto the surface.

"Come on, show me. Show me what's happening," I said.

I dabbed my finger a few times into the rainbow of colours glistening atop the surface, to create chaos, so that the forces may guide me.

"Show me the future," I commanded, "show me a future where I do nothing to stop them."

I leant forwards on my arms and watched and waited and waited some more.

After a time, the swirls gradually steadied and began to form. Form the shapes of two lovers.

They slow-danced together, intertwined, momentarily coiling as one, then parting again.

A small island of grease and oil drifted from one of the figures as it peeled away from the other. It fluoresced with viscera and seemed to have limbs, tiny limbs.

"They're going to have a child?" I simpered—shocked by the vision. "If I do nothing, they'll have a child?"

A gritting, chalkboard and fingernail squeal filled my eardrums, then I realised my teeth were grinding, grinding to dust at the final indignity.

We'd been trying for a child for years without success. And now, she was going to get fucked by that cunt of a man and bear 'his' child.

My hands clamped the side of the butler-sink and cracked with anger as they gripped it.

I began panting through my teeth, breath whistling and rage spitting through the gaps in my gnashing jawline.

"Yooooou fffffucking wanker!" I seethed.

My mind was finally made, and nothing could change it—'ever'.

I grasped the rim of the washing up bowl and hurled it across the room.

It splashed up the wall, and the plates inside shattered against the exposed brickwork, crashing to the floor.

I noticed a framed photo hanging right next to the impact, a new photo I'd not seen there before.

I walked across to look at it.

It was one of the photos from the garden party at Kirsty's. I hadn't even noticed that Marianna had hung it.

It had her and me and 'Mark' in the background, looking smug and handsome.

168

I felt my shuddering lip curl hard into my nose and I drove my fist into the glass and held it there, pinning it against the wall.

The blood from my knuckles began to seep through the fractures and meniscus across the image.

I twisted my anger, drilling my loathing for that man into the hateful image.

My blood ran thick, dripping down the wall.

I withdrew the fist and the picture slid down and broke apart on the floor.

I hocked up a jaw full of phlegm and spat it with force onto the shattered pieces.

It lay there, like a mocking metaphor for my relationship.

I picked the fragments of glass from my shredded knuckles and wrapped them in tissue.

I decided, I didn't want to do this 'thing' up in the loft space. I wanted to do it in my basement, my workshop, my womb. The one place I'd felt the most happiness in my entire life.

I needed to move the altar down into the cellar. It was in three sections, and each one was incredibly heavy.

But I 'wanted' to do it. I 'needed' to do it. This was just my house now, and the only reason it was in the loft space in the first place, was because it was a secret, a dirty, filthy secret, and if I hadn't needed to, I'd always have housed it in the basement.

And the fact is, it's better to have an altar grounded—at one with the earth it feeds—the energies it controls and influences plugged directly to the conduit that projects them out, to control the destinies of those you've marked.

So, down it would come. "My fucking house now," I muttered.

It took the majority of five hours of toil to dismantle the altar and transport its not inconsiderable mass down the loft ladder and both staircases, using boards, ropes and sleds made of old carpet.

I mixed cement and bedded the blocks down onto their new home, centre of the cold, stone-slab flooring, making sure the cabalistic markings I'd chiselled into the surface all those years ago lined up precisely.

I stepped back to admire my work; it looked good there—gothic and in keeping, not the sore thumb it had always been in the loft space like a priest in a strip club.

I pushed the benches and units clear of the main event sat centre stage.

They circled the perimeter of the cellar with their backs to the wall, looking in awe at the stone monolith growing majestically from the ground.

I swept the floor in readiness for the markings, finding years of dropped pieces from all I'd ever made down there, and by the end, I virtually had a whole marionette in kit-form lying on the side.

I carefully boxed the parts and tidied them away.

I began to relish not having to hide myself away. Having the house all to my own for the first time ever.

Would I have traded that for never having had Marianna in my life? No, never. But witchcraft had been 'my' mistress, 'my' dirty secret for all those years, hidden out of sight for all of our years together.

Did that make my reaction to her infidelity wrong, or unfair? No, it didn't. I'd only hidden 'my' secrets because they were misunderstood, not because to know them would've destroyed a person—as hers had me.

It took roughly another six hours on my hands and knees painting the floor with the relevant script and interlinking geometry.

An all-encompassing circle gave home to a large pentagram, Arabic and runic symbology filling every corner of every interlocking shape, like the scribblings of an expressive child let loose with a marker pen.

Tired—I struggled from the floor and examined my handiwork.

It was art, and I felt strangely proud of what I'd created, what I'd managed to do in just a day. But I'd never have that moment of pleasure and satisfaction that comes from showing your creations, your 'art' to another. This particular 'piece', was just for me.

Wearily—I climbed the stone staircase and crossed the kitchen.

I swung open the cupboard above the kettle and lifted onto my toes, but there was no salt in there. Over those couple of tumultuous months, I must have used it all.

Marianna had always wondered just why there was so much salt in the house. It was a crucial substance in the practice of all things magic. It cleansed and protected but could also be used to block, or unravel another's attempts to influence 'your' life, and I needed more, to pour the final ring of protection around the new home of my altar-stone.

I checked the time, grabbed the keys off the side and left through the back door.

There was a small corner shop a short walk from the cottage that stayed open until eight.

I strode there and arrived with three minutes to spare.

The owner, Graham, was straightening the store in readiness for closure, putting everything to bed for the night.

I puffed past the small, brass bell as the door clipped it, ringing my arrival. "Hey, Graham." I wheezed. I was tired, and my breathing was heavy.

He turned, peering at my last-minute arrival over the top of his horn-rimmed spectacles. It took him a moment to recognise me, then his face brightened to the recognition.

"Helllllo, Sam, how's things? Haven't seen you in a while," he chirped.

He was an eternally happy man—good to visit when you're feeling down. But I wasn't feeling down at that moment, my feelings were more 'determined', and I needed salt.

"I won't keep you, Graham, I just need some salt."

He laughed, slapped the till shut and rounded the counter to collect one of the large, six-kilo bags that I was pretty sure he only got in because of me.

"I've never known someone use as much salt as you. What the hell do you do with it?" His tone was subtly derisive, but I didn't take it to heart, it was just his way.

"Oh, I-I use it as a setting agent when I'm dyeing fabrics, you know, for my puppets. 'And' for cooking, of course."

"Oh." He laughed. "I thought you had a secret Biltong factory squirrelled away in your basement, or something."

"My basement?" I said. I couldn't remember ever telling him I had a basement. I purposely avoided doing so to locals, to prevent curiosity bringing forth the question 'can I come down sometime and take a look around?'

"How did you know I had a basement?" I asked.

"Marianna told me. She says you're always down there, working on your puppets. She says the things you make are fantastic. She's always singing your praises, mate. I'd love to come over see it sometime."

And there it was, 'that' question.

An image of Marianna, embracing Mark, pressing her red, glossed lips against his, popped with the force of a flash bulb into my thoughts.

It took me out of the shop to a darker place. A place I was sinking to with increasing regularity.

I must have blanked out of the conversation for a brief moment, because I re-emerged to the sight of Graham clicking his fingers towards me.

I was driving my teeth hard together. "Are you all right?" he asked. He looked genuinely concerned.

Another image hit my thoughts like a bolt of electricity, of her, riding me, sitting high in my vision, her firm, sweat beaded body rippling as she rose and fell, and…

I shook myself clear of the visions. Graham looked concerned. "I'm sorry," I mumbled, "I've—I've had a busy day, I didn't realise how tired I was."

"That's okay. That's okay," he muttered, "it's easily done. Are you going to be all right getting home?"

"Oh God, yeah. I'm okay now. I just had, I dunno, a moment." I smiled wide to waylay the worry masking his face.

I slipped my card from my back pocket and tapped it on the reader held out towards me. "I'm fine now, Graham," I assured him.

I took up the bag of salt and smiled. "I'll see you soon, and thanks for the salt."

He didn't reply at first, just watched me backing away with a perplexed look on his face. "Yeah. Sure. You take care now," he muttered, sounding pensive.

I left the store, the tiny, brass bell ringing my departure.

I had the salt, and in addition—as a bonus—an alibi.

I dropped off the step and my eyes turned to the sky. It looked about five shades darker than when I went in.

There were angry, black clouds hanging ominously above, looking pregnant with rain and thunder—but I already knew there was a storm coming.

I made it back just before the downpour started and descended the staircase carrying the bag of salt and the old pair of scissors I'd used to clip Marianna's hair from her beautiful young head all those years ago.

Their involvement seemed, somehow, right—there at the beginning. There at the end—full circle.

I sheared the corner off the bag and began pouring a wall of salt crystals around the perimeter of my newly laid ceremonial circle.

"This is my circle and this shall protect me. This is my circle and this shall protect me. This is my circle and this shall protect me," I chanted, in my monotonous, monophonic tone, as I formed the ring of glistening white sand.

I kept looping until the bag ran empty, and I tossed it aside.

I placed the large, black candle and my Athame—a ritualistic dagger—on top the stone monolith and hung in the damp, earthy stench of the setting cement inspecting all I'd done.

My phone rang out, and I looked around to locate where the sound was coming from. Then I remembered I'd left it on the kitchen table.

I carefully stepped over the wall of salt so as to not break it and ran upstairs to answer the call.

I grabbed the phone off the table. Marianna's name was flashing on the screen. I thumbed the answer button and carried it to my ear. "Hello?" I said, sounding weirdly apprehensive.

"Helloooooo," came her voice, happy and bright, "it's me, your dishy girlfriend."

I didn't know how I felt; I'd bizarrely forgotten she'd likely ring at some point, and I wasn't ready for it.

"Em…Hi," I replied, feeling oddly disconnected.

I could hear her laughing on the other end of the line. "Are you all right? How much heroine have you had *this* time?"

"Hm? Oh. Sorry, I'm miles away. Where are you?"

She paused. "I'm in Disney World, Florida. It's great, there's a massive mouse," she said, "where do you think I am, I'm at the hotel in Coventry; it's nice."

"Of course. Yeah. Of course, you are. Sorry."

She went quiet on the line. "Are you okay?" she asked with genuine concern in her voice. "You seem, different. I thought you'd be happy to hear from me?"

I finally managed to snap out of my trance. "Of course. Of course, I am. I'm sorry; I've just been busy today; I didn't realise how late it was. So the hotel's nice, yeah?"

"Yes, it's very nice. It has a *huge* queen-sized bed and a corner bath with bubble jets."

Her rippling stomach and wet lips burst into my thoughts again, but this time, they were sat atop Mark. Riding. Grinding. Legs spread open. "You're in separate rooms, right?" I asked, not thinking—a Freudian blurt from an insecure mouth.

She laughed again, but this time, it felt more like she was ridiculing me. "You fool," she slurred, laughing again. "Of course, we're in separate rooms."

I felt slightly paranoid about my mood. Inexplicably, I still seemed to care how I was perceived in her catlike eyes, and I feared parting with her thinking she was moving on to better pastures.

I wanted our final conversation to be a good one, that left her wondering what she was doing to jeopardise such a strong and good relationship.

I needed to end the call and do it properly later. "Look, I'm sorry, honey, I'll call you back in a bit when I'm not so distracted. Is that okay?"

The line went quiet again. The answer I finally got was—unfortunately—just what I needed to hear.

"Oh. Well. Can we leave it until tomorrow now, sweetheart? Mark's coming over and wants to talk over some stuff, so it's best I'm not disturbed for a bit, not while he's here. Is that okay?"

I dropped the phone from my mouth and boiled. I felt like a grenade, pin pulled, lever spinning through the air, fuse fizzing and ready to detonate.

I took a long breath and exhaled the rage away. "Of course. Of course. Not a problem. I'll leave you two alone then, have a good night."

"Ah, thanks, honey, you're good to me. I think he's bringing a bottle over, so we might be some time," she said.

She seemed to let go a giggle, I could hear her, but I'm not sure I was supposed to hear it. Was he already there? Listening to our conversation? Laughing?

I managed to hold it in. "That's good," I said, trying to sound calm. "Okay then, I'll leave you two to it. Goodbye."

"Bye, love," she said and rang off.

"Goodbye," I said again, to the closed connection. "I've loved you," I added.

Calmly, I placed the phone back down on the table and wandered into the living room.

I had a fire on the go, and it was just starting to die down.

I took a knee and tossed a few more logs onto the glowing embers.

They began to crackle and fizz the moment they landed. They had been drying for weeks at the side of the hearth in readiness for winter.

I was originally to wait until the next day to do what I needed to do, but I saw no point in delaying it now. The timing felt right, and I craved freedom from my pain.

I descended into the cellar, opened the hidden draw and carefully carried the marionettes of the traitorous stains on my happiness across to the altar, hanging them from puppet-stands I had in readiness.

I climbed the stairs to our bedroom, took up Marianna's antique hand-mirror from her dressing table, then carried it back down to the kitchen.

I pulled out the cutlery draw, took up the potato peeler in my fingers, then rolled the tee-towel into a rope and bit down on it.

I snorted a few times to ready myself for the pain that was coming, clamped my jaw hard onto the towel and pressed the blade of the peeler hard against my wrist. With a determined growl through the musty weave of the cloth, I began dragging it up my forearm.

The blade sliced into the surface and started peeling a slither of flesh from my clenched fist arm—farming a ribbon of my own blood-soaked skin as I dragged it to the pit of my elbow.

I chomped down hard onto the cloth and twisted the blade up to cut the ribbon free. The towel fell from my grimacing mouth and unfurled at my feet.

I leant on the counter, reeling in pain, feeling close to blacking out, but somehow, I managed to hold it together.

My arm started leeching blood. It dripped to my fingertips and poured onto the floorboards.

I staggered to the sink and grabbed a glass off the drainer and dangled my fingers above it, catching the thick, crimson treacle.

I stretched over and took a sock from the washing basket on the side and snipped the foot off with the scissors that were still in my pocket, slipping it over my arm to help quell the bleeding.

The water ran red as I washed the blood from my fingers, before I took up the mirror and the slither of skin and carried them down to the altar.

I lit the candle and placed the linguini of skin over to one side.

Taking the Athame in my hand, I stabbed it hard into the centre of the mirror, shattering it into a thousand tiny shards emanating from the tip like a spider's web.

I thumbed one of the slithers free of the mirror and carefully placed it against the right palm of Marianna's puppet.

It lay like a dagger in the tiny hand, and I began binding it in place with the ribbon of skin.

Chapter Fifteen

The Performance

MARIANNA PASCAL glanced at the tiny, mother-of-pearl facia of her watch, then looked across at the large, queen-sized bed beckoning to her from the farthest side of her plush, hotel suite.

The day had been long, and the steady, uneventful drive to Coventry had eased her into some variety of torpor that she hadn't yet fully woken from, and the idea of crawling beneath the pure white sheets of the huge, overstuffed bed laid out before her was as close to irresistible as anything could be.

But she had to fight the temptation just a little bit longer. Mark—her boss—was on his way to join her in her room, apparently, with a bottle of wine in tow.

She stepped into the bathroom and presented herself in the mirror, the fluorescent ring-light bleaching her features to vague shadows of what was there, leaving only her eyes and full, red lips visible through the stark, white luminance.

She leaned into her reflection, rolling her face to all angles, inspecting herself.

She pawed her slender fingers at the laughter-lines time had formed off the Egyptian sweep of her eyes, then decided they were part of her face now and leant back to consider the bigger picture.

She took up a lipstick from the countertop, uncapped it and gave it a twist.

Carefully, her experienced hand traced the crimson bullet around the contours of her full, bowed lip-line, then rolled them together, recapping the stick with a jaunty slap of the palm.

She smacked her lips apart and smiled at herself, please with what she saw looking back at her.

From early childhood on, she'd always been a supremely attractive female, and as the years rolled by, that beauty remained and arguably improved as she grew comfortable in her own skin.

A rare and extraordinary beauty possessed only by a few but admired by many, if not all.

179

There was a faint knocking at the door. She glanced across at the sound.

Quickly, she tousled her tumbling hair with her fingertips and turned to answer it—stretching back to switch off the light and pull the bathroom door shut behind her.

She swung the door open to reveal her boss, Mark, stood in the corridor, rattling a bottle of Brut Imperial out towards her.

"It's champagne o'clock," he said, with an air of celebration, stepping into the room.

He'd changed into fresh clothes—the long, working day and the journey there having taken its toll on the previous outfit.

He had on light, linen slacks and a tight, fitted shirt—midnight blue with a sheen that gave it an appearance of silk, sleeves rolled to his elbows, the three top buttons undone.

She'd also changed, into a subtly gothic slim black skirt and a black, laced top, its paucity of colour allowing her natural beauty to sing its existence and light up the room.

She also had on her black, patent, three-inch heels, purely to make sense of the outfit, but she sorely wished they were her soft, fur-lined slippers and couldn't help darting a look in their direction, parked neatly on the shelf of the wardrobe in readiness, next to her case that housed her favourite pyjamas.

Marianna stepped back from the door and swung an arm to invite him in.

Mark accepted, stepping past her, his eyes absorbing the details of the room to compare it to his own.

"I think yours is slightly bigger than mine?" he said.

"Oh—well—if you'd like to swap. I don't—"

He scoffed a laugh. "Don't be daft. The beautiful, gorgeous, elegant lady *should* have the bigger room," he said, with a nonchalant turn, a smile and a flash of the brows.

She blushed and smiled coyly.

Mark giggled, enjoying the fruits of the reaction he'd managed to orchestrate.

There had been a small round table and two tub chairs folded neatly in the corner of the room, and Marianna had had the foresight to draw them further into the space in readiness for Mark's arrival.

She'd also experimented with every combination possible with the multiple islands of light dotted about the room, until she'd found one that—to her—felt cosy and intimate.

"I got us a couple of glasses from the bar downstairs," she said, pointing to the flutes sat in readiness on the table.

"God, I didn't even think of that, I was just going to use the teacups or swig straight from the bottle," he said, jokingly but meaning it. They laughed.

"Pikey," Marianna said.

He shrugged a 'whatever' and smiled—enjoying the friendly ridicule.

He relished the times outside of the work environment, where they could interact more as friends and break free the boundary that naturally exists when others are in your pay.

He also had good reason to desire building a closer bond with Marianna, a reason he was yet to reveal.

"Jesus, you look amazing," he said, as Marianna strode majestically through one of the islands of light she'd orchestrated. "I've always meant to ask you something but never have."

"Ask me? Ask me what?" she replied—curious.

He picked his words. "*Do*—you actually, *know* how beautiful you are, or do you have to take people's word for it?"

"Mark," she complained, with a swoop in her voice, "what are you doing? Stop trying to embarrass me."

"No. No, I'm being serious—this fascinates me—*Do* people who look the way *you* do, *actually* know? Actually know that you're beautiful to look at?"

Marianna rolled her countenance despairingly. "I. I don't know. A bit. I suppose. You know." She turned to face him, fist planted firmly on her hip. "Anyway, how would you know?"

"How would I know what?"

"That I'm attractive?"

He chuckled, then smirked, dismissively. "Trust me, I know." He laughed.

"Are you going to pop that bottle of plonk or not? I'm dying of thirst here," she complained—the employer/employee divide all but dissolved to nothing for the night.

"All right, all right. Here we go," he said—stepping to the table.

He skinned the foil from the cork and began un-twisting the cage.

He shifted a sly, knowing look out of the corner of his eyes across at Marianna, as he worked to liberate the carbonated wine. "She knows," he proclaimed—with a knowing grin.

She blushed for the second time in just two minutes and shook her head in comic despair.

They sat with their drinks, and Mark lifted a toast. "To a fun couple of days, you and me."

Marianna didn't really know how to respond; she'd never been for a weekend away like this before, so didn't know what to expect, let alone know what would constitute 'fun' on a weekend like this.

So she just nodded and took a long sip of her drink. "Mmm, that's nice," she said, as the bubbles fizzed her throat awake.

"I had it chilling overnight and brought it in one of those cooler bag thingies," he said, "Brut's my favourite."

He drew in half of the flute and placed the glass on the table.

He tilted a pensive look past his shoulder to the floor. "I've been wondering whether to bring this up now, or wait until after we're back. But if I'm honest, I'm not sure *what* the best time would be to talk about—well, *this*," he said, looking considerate of the words he was obviously taking great pains to choose with wisdom.

"What is it?" Marianna asked—feeling slightly concerned at the reluctant tone in his voice. She could find no clues in his manner and had no information to even throw an educated guess at it.

He continued to talk with his eyes averted; she could see him working to craft his sentences with care. "I guess, you've been wondering, *why* I've been training you up as a stylist. Well, at least giving you a good all-round knowledge of exactly *what* styling entails."

"Well, yeah. I, I had been wondering," she said, confirming his notion.

He paused for his thoughts again. She could see him racked in contemplation of how much to say.

"I've bought another property, in Stock Norton, and my plan is to open it as a second salon, and I'll be needing someone to manage it for me." He finally bent his gaze her way. "And I couldn't think of anyone better to do that, than *you*."

Marianna sat stunned by his revelation. The gossip machine at the salon had seriously failed her on this one.

"You've bought another place?"

He nodded, eyes locked on hers to try and gauge a reaction. "The builders are in there *now*, sorting it out. That's why, of late, I've been having to pop out from time to time, to go and see how they're getting on."

"And does anyone else at the salon know?"

"Nope. You're the first person from work I've told."

Marianna felt strangely honoured. "Wow," she muttered under the weight of her thoughts.

"The way I would *like* to do it, would be for *you*, to earn a percentage of the takings, so if the salon does well, so do you. But you'd be earning at least double what you're getting now to start with but probably quite a bit more once you've filled the client book, and it's a quarter full already." He shrugged and held it. "So? What do you think? Interested?"

She sat pondering the notion but didn't really need to; she already had the answer perched on her tongue. "Yes," she said, "if you're sure, of course, I am. Yes."

Mark beamed and rose to receive the hug Marianna was already rising to administer. "That's great," he said, as he engulfed her happiness in his arms. "It gives me comfort to know the place will be in good hands. So, these next two days, take it *aaaall* in."

"I will," she said, "I'll be all eyes and ears, I promise."

"That's brilliant, that makes me so happy; there's no one else I could think that I'd want to ask. So I'm made up. Seriously."

Samuel popped into her thoughts and hung there in her mind. "Mark. While you're here, can I ask your advice on something?"

Mark read the worry in her voice as it vibrated through his shoulder. It seemed to him—genuine. "Of course, you can, anything. What's the matter? Is it about my offer?" he said, as they took to their seats again.

"Noooo, no. Not at all. And it's not *really* a problem like *that*, I just need some advice, about something I want to do."

"Okay, well, go ahead, I'll do what I can to help."

He took up the bottle and topped up their glasses. "Go for it."

It was now Marianna's turn to carefully construct her sentences. She took a moment to arrange her words. "I'm sure you were probably aware that me and Sam recently had—well—problems."

He nodded. "I knew something went on, but I'm not sure what."

Marianna sighed. "It was just something I probably over-reacted to, and it got a bit out of hand. Then of course, Jennifer took—her—" She stopped to take a breath. "Then, the Jennifer thing—happened, and it put things into perspective for me. And ever since that day, Sam's been *so* good to me, *so* lovely, and I've finally come to realise how lucky I am to have him. To have someone *like* him."

Mark smiled. He thought Sam a bit of an oddball when they'd met at the party, but he could see how happy he made Marianna, and that was enough to make him look favourably upon him.

"That's great, so what's the issue? What did you want my advice on?"

A tear curled from the corner of Marianna's eye and meandered down her cheek. "Is it considered wrong, o-or improper, for a woman to ask a man to marry her?"

"You want to *marry* him? As in, get *married?*" he asked.

She nodded. "Yes. I love him."

He leant back out of the conversation to formulate an answer. "Well, *I* don't see why not. It's a modern world after all, equal rights and all that. And *my* partner's just asked *me* to marry him, and he considers *me* to be the husband of *our* strange little relationship. So is that really any different?"

Marianna's face washed with joy; this was news to her. "And you said yes?" she asked.

"Of course, I did; he's lovely. You bet I said yes."

"Oh my God. Wow, I didn't even know you were still seeing anyone. That's fantastic," she enthused, leaning forwards into another embrace. "Why didn't you say anything at the salon?"

"Well, you know me, I'm quite secretive, as poofs go."

"Wowwww. I'm so happy for you," she said, her angelic voice ringing loud in his ear.

She sat again and looked him dead in the face; she had all of his attention. "There's actually a reason I wanted to ask Sam now; I don't have much time, you see."

"What do you mean, you don't have much time?" he said with a flicker of his brows.

"You see. I'm. I'm pregnant."

Mark's face fell open. "What? And he's—"

She nodded and smiled. "The father? Yes. I didn't think we could, but I am."

"And he doesn't know?"

She shook her head. "Not yet."

"Shit!" he said, rocking back. It felt weirdly like 'he' was receiving news of his 'own' child, and he felt somehow—invested.

"I'd make sure it impacts the salon as little as possible; I don't want to be home for ages or anything."

"Oh—forget that. That's not an issue. You've always been a good worker, so we'll work around you," he said, to alleviate her concern.

Mark's eyes gravitated to Marianna's side, his brows pinched, something out of place confused him.

Marianna wondered what had drawn his attention and turned her eyes to follow his gaze.

They both sat staring at Marianna's arm, held out to the side, floating ethereally mid-air, like someone was holding it, and to Mark's mind, it was something she was obviously not doing herself.

Her hand still held the glass, the champagne spilling out onto the carpet.

His confused eyes darted between her shocked face and the floating arm.

Marianna tried lowering it back to her side, but it seemed paralysed, numb, and she literally had no control over it.

"W-W-What's happening?" she said, the stammering panic in her voice obvious, "W-W-W-Why can't I move it?"

Mark could see her trying in vain. The sight unnerved him. He wondered if she was having some kind of stroke? *Is this what that looks like?* he thought. Marianna began to weep.

"I-I don't know? A-Aren't you doing that?" he asked, the oddness of the sight before him adding a tremble to his voice.

She shook her head frantically. "No. No. No. No, I'm not. What's happening to me?"

Her arm began to fold inwards, carrying her hand to her face. Then it extended violently, smashing her fist into the mirror on the wall.

It shattered, and shards of glass ricocheted across the table. "What are you doing? What the fuck are you doing!" Mark screamed, as he jumped back, sending his seat flying across the room.

He looked back at Marianna, who was now holding a slither of the mirror, gripped tightly in her bleeding fingers. "H-H-Help meeeeeeee," she pleaded, from a face prostrate with desperation, powerless to stop herself.

Her eyes caught sight of a face reflected in the shard of glass as it passed her eyes, a stranger's face, neither Mark's, nor her own, but the face of an impish demon with cruelty in its eyes, peek-a-boo peering from behind her shoulders, teeth chattering some form of warped pleasure.

Her hand suddenly dragged the slither of glass across her throat. She felt the pop as it broke the surface of her skin and sliced across her neck.

A pumping warmth began trickling down her chest, and Mark ran in to try and quell the flow…

Samuel Grant stood looming over the marionette hanging from his fingers, completing a long, steady swipe of the string that controls its tiny hand.

"Bleed, bitch," he murmured. "Fucking bleeeeeed."

He completed the motion, his lip quivering his disgust and resentment. Then carefully, lay the puppet down on the altar.

He averted his attention to the next marionette on his agenda—the one of the lover. The one he felt 'real' spite towards.

He unhooked it and lowered it onto its feet.

He slowly closed his eyes and opened the floodgates of his mind, losing a torrent of his worst thoughts and intentions that raged like a ruptured dam through his jealous imagination.

His lip began to curl, trembling with ultimate loathing.

He opened his eyes again, anger filling his face.

"Youuuuu, fuckinnnng, cunnnnnnnnnt!" he slurred, grasping the controls of the puppet in his bared teeth, biting down hard onto the control-sticks and sliding his clawed grip down the strings to the marionette hanging helplessly below his grimacing face…

Mark knelt before Marianna, panic freezing his thoughts.

She lay slumped against the wall like a dropped ragdoll, gluts of blood heaving from her throat.

He tried in vain to cup his hands across the gaping maw, but it just kept emptying her life through his fingers and down her chest.

"W-Why?" he sobbed, helpless to stop the flow. "Why would you do that!?"

Marianna's vision began to blur, her expression emotionless in the air of unreality of all that was happening.

She could feel herself emptying.

Mark suddenly lifted to his feet, a bizarrely unnatural motion, pulled up by some invisible force like he was on a rope.

Marianna could see confusion and fear in his face, even through the films of drying tears and her blood-starved vision.

His head spun, disorientated, looking for who it was who'd grabbed him, but there was no one else there in the room with them. They were alone.

He suddenly stiffened and began to scream. Not a manly roar but the high-pitched squeal of a schoolgirl…

Samuel Grant's face contorted as he began twisting the puppet in his hateful grip, like he was wringing water from a towel, the hatred in his face seeping down his arms and into his fingers, as he mercilessly wound the marionette in his white-knuckled grip…

Mark felt like he was trapped in a tube, unable to move, his whole body coiling up like a spring.

He felt his stomach muscles twist tight, unable to stretch any further, then begin to tear.

He screamed the scream of a helpless, dying man, as his chest slowly turned to face fully backwards.

Marianna watched the blurred, corkscrew figure of Mark through clouding eyes, suspended mid-air, his body winding up like a candy cane.

She could hear the cracking of his bones in her receding consciousness but wasn't sure if any of this was real or not. It all looked far too other-worldly to actually be happening.

All felt like a dream as she floated back away from the real world. Her slouched body emptying. Emptying. Emptying.

There was a loud, hollow, woody crack, as Mark's spine relented to the invisible force and life left his body.

His crushed remains dropped to the carpet like a wet flannel, a lifeless bag of shattered bones and torn sinew.

"Maaaaaaaaaaaaaark," Marianna wept, as she exhaled her last, gurgling breath.

She looked on what remained of him lying dead on the floor, the last thing she would ever see through vision rapidly tunnelling to a single point of light.

A frantic knocking sound began emanating from the door of her room and receding voices shouting something she couldn't quite make out in the haze.

With the final, wilting strength she had left, Marianna lifted a hand to cup her belly. Her baby. 'Their' baby.

Her hand rested on a wet, bib of coagulating plasma. "Samuelllllllll," she mouthed with barely a sound.

Her open eyes dried over. The last of the blood seeped from her gaping throat, and she drifted away into final sleep.

Chapter Sixteen

The End

I HELD THE TWO halves of Mark's marionette in my hands, the performance was over, and the feelings in the aftermath of my actions were strangely unnerving.

The energies that I could feel through my fingertips before had dissipated. They'd gone.

I don't really understand 'why' I was surprised, that was my intention all along. But it just felt uncanny to actually feel the life dissipate through my grip and bear witness its passing.

But then I realised, I'd felt a similar thing before, when I'd sacrificed the dog, and it had finally succumbed to my efforts.

I dropped the splintered remains onto the ground and took up the puppet of Marianna, holding it still in my hands, trying to feel a semblance of an aura. But I couldn't, I felt nothing; it too was devoid of life.

But even more than that, the whole 'house' felt somehow empty, as if the life-force left by Marianna's presence there in the cottage had died along with her.

And that's when I knew for sure—something important was no longer in my world, in my life, 'part' of my life, and tragically, I knew that it was 'I' that was the cause and the culprit.

A feeling of desolation began infesting the cellar, infesting 'me'. "What have I done?" I asked the marionettes watching from the side-lines. Their faces looking cold and unfriendly, their tiny glass eyes scolding of my actions.

And why wouldn't they, I'd just used two of their kind to do something deplorable and diabolical, and forgiveness wasn't in their gift.

I finally realised 'just' what it was I'd done—I'd destroyed the only thing I'd ever lived for; I'd ever cared for; I'd ever loved and nurtured. The one and only driving force and real meaning to my otherwise lonely existence.

I panicked and fumbled at my pockets for my phone.

I'd never had any of my magic fail to produce a result in all the years I'd been using it, using it to correct my failings as a human being trying to exist in a society that favoured others.

But I hoped upon hope and prayed that this time—just this once—it hadn't worked.

I found my phone and stuttered my fingers at the screen, trying to bring up Marianna's number.

I finally managed to open it and hit 'call'.

The phone began to ring, and I held my breath, listening to the double tone reciprocate, over and over and over, unanswered.

Then the double tone ceased, and I assumed it had gone to voicemail.

What message would I leave? I wasn't supposed to be ringing her. Then I had a thought, I could pretend it was a pocket call, a mistake. Easily done.

Then a voice spoke on the other end of the line. A man's voice?

"Hello. Who is this calling?" it asked.

"Erm? Well, what? M-My name's Samuel Grant. Who is this? Is that Mark?" I asked.

"No, sir, who's phone is that you're ringing?"

"Marianna. Marianna Pascal. *Who* is this?" I insisted.

"Do you know the—do you know Miss Pascal, personally?"

"Yes!" I barked. "I'm her partner. *Who* the hell *are* you?" I asked again—losing patience.

The line went quiet. I could hear the muffled murmurings of voices in the background and the creaking of plastic of a phone being held by a hand covering the mouthpiece.

The line brightened again. "Em, Mr Grant. My name is PC Taylor. Wh-Where abouts are you at the moment? We need to send someone over to see yo—"

I quickly punched the phone off. "Oh shit," I exhaled. "Oh God, no!"

My phone began to ring, it was Marianna's number showing. I quickly grasped the handset in my shaking hands and snapped it in two and threw the pieces across the cellar.

A turbulent feeling boiled through my feet and up my legs, sizzling through me like an erupting volcano, and I screamed. I screamed and screamed and screamed until my lungs were empty and crowding my throat.

"Mmmmmmaaaaaaariaaaaannaaaaaaaaaaaaaa!" I wailed. "Oh Jesus, Mariannaaaa, Oh Christ in Heaven please. No. Oh God in Heaven, no. I love you, what have I done? I'm sorry, I'm so, so sorry," I cried—and cried and cried some more. Crying until my batteries ran empty.

I had nothing left. No reason to live, no one to love me, and nothing to love— I'd just killed that—and my previous arguments that she was deserving of my actions crumbled to nothing in the light of my remorse and the cold, crushing grip of reality.

Reality—something I'd avoided for most of my life. Maybe if I'd allowed just one foot to remain planted firmly in the realm of the real world I was so incompetent at inhabiting, maybe none of this would have happened.

But happen it had, and I knew what I needed to do to end the pain of my inability to cope.

I sat on the cold, stone floor, huddled in the corner of the workshop, the marionette of my beautiful, wonderful Marianna resting on my shoulder, hands stroking her tiny back.

I rocked in my pain and held her until my tears ran dry and I could sob no more.

I staggered to my feet and lay Marianna gently back on the altar, bowing a kiss to her tiny, carved lips.

A single tear fell from my eye and splashed onto her face.

We shared our final sadness.

I reached through my wall of puppets and took up the one of me, lifting it over the judgmental gathering to the front.

I stared into it. It stared back. And despite having made it ten years earlier, it still looked eerily like me.

Standing, regarding my diminutive, replica features gave me a similar sensation to when I would look down upon myself asleep in bed, when I used to make mirth projecting myself into the astral plane during my twenties, when the experiences witchcraft could gift me were still new and exciting.

I opened a drawer of one of my cabinets and took out a half-round palm chisel and began gouging at the heart of the diminutive me.

I blew away the shavings, then peeled the sock from my forearm.

I dug my fingernails in deep and began to scratch at the wound. It started to bleed again, droplets of blood trickling along my arm like an escalator to my shaking fingertips.

I held them above the puppet, and the plasma began to fill the hole I'd gouged into the tiny body, soaking the fibres of the desiccated timbers.

"Everything I am, is in you. All you experience, I do too. You control me. You own me. You *are* me. And you—this poppet lying before me—*are* my destiny," I recited, over and over and over again, as the cherry red fluid drowned the wood.

My blood began to coagulate, and the drips turned to gelatinous beads dangling from my fingertips.

I smeared them on my jeans and took up the marionette in my blood-gloved hand.

"Mmmmmmmariiiiiiiii—" I wept, as I began ascending steps, stopping midway to take a last, long look back at my workshop, my home—my womb.

I tried to smile for the happy times, but I couldn't.

How I wish I could take back my actions and see her again, even if it was for just one more time.

The puppets seemed to have turned to watch me leave. "I'm sorry," I sobbed, "please, forgive me."

But they just watched me over cold shoulders, shunning my actions.

"Goodbye," I said, turning to continue the climb.

My legs felt heavy and leaden with guilt. I stepped through into the kitchen and hung in the emptiness for a moment, feeling numb—I'd lost everything.

I heard a pop and a crackle from the living room; I turned and walked inside, dragging the puppet behind me.

The fire was still burning bright, glowing as red as Hell.

Marianna's face flashed into my thoughts. Smiling, laughing—beautiful.

I walked to the fireplace and stooped to poke the embers. They erupted to the agitation and began throwing animated flames up the chimney stack.

I stood again, then saw a familiar face reflected in the mirror above the mantle, watching me from the unlit corner of the room, up by the ceiling.

It was Aishma. He'd come for me.

He leant out from the wall, carrying his face into the light.

He grinned at the sight of my grief, as his limp, black tongue lowered out of his open mouth like a wet rope, the tip oscillating, tasting the remorse flavouring the air.

I could see horns clashing behind his thin, skeletal shoulders, as his eyes beckoned me to do what was in my heart.

My eyes left the mirror, and I tossed the marionette into the fire.

The lines caught first and fizzed like fuses, flames chasing along their lengths until they'd turned to tracks of black powder crisscrossing the glowing embers.

I looked on, strangely detached from what was happening, like I was watching it all unfold on a cinema screen.

Then the warmth came. First in my legs and lower back, then began to spread across my entire body.

The warmth became heat. The heat became flames. My jaw started burning, ribbons of fire licking around my chin and into my nostrils.

I tried snorting the heat away, but it just deflected it into my eyes.

I shut them tight and my lids singed.

The pain set in. Scalding, searing pain. The smell of burning hair filled the room.

I could feel my legs incinerating in the chimneys of my trouser-legs, until they too caught fire and began carrying the inferno up my body.

I began to shudder and seethe as the fire turned my skin molten, and I could feel myself cooking inside.

Then, the pain subsided? The eye of the storm. And I remember thinking— *My layer of nerve-ending must have burnt away, is that why I can feel nothing anymore?*

I stood ablaze in the living room, pondering these thoughts, calmly and with cogent consideration.

I felt a jolt in my head. I think I must have dropped to my knees, but I had no feeling left in my legs to know.

I tried opening my eyes to see, but the infernal heat hit them, and they ruptured.

I felt the hot flames curling into my eye sockets.

Then it stopped.

And what of me now? What became of such a man?

Well. I reside in a place between darkness and light. A world without time, only eternity.

To my left, a brightness so fierce I can scarcely see it. To my right, a faint glow, where streams of the unfortunate come and pass me by to transcend realities and become as one with the brightness I cannot reach and dare not look to see.

For I am 'Samuel', the underworld prince of jealousy, wrath and disdain.

My heart is as black as ink, and my methods of retribution—bleak.

Those who feel the need, can call on me, and I will come, to fulfil their darkest desires and feed off the sweetmeats of their ill-will and detestation.

But, a warning to the curious. The piper requires payment, to feed my unquenchable thirst for vengeance.

And the fee for my services?—Is you.